THE CHRISTMAS CONQUEST

CLAIRE DELACROIX

DEBORAH A. COOKE

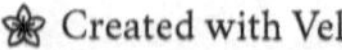 Created with Vellum

THE LADIES' ESSENTIAL GUIDE
TO THE ART OF SEDUCTION

REGENCY ROMANCES

The Ladies' Essential Guide to the Art of Seduction is a series of Regency romances. In each story, a marriage in dire straits is rescued by the lady's consultation of Miss Esmeralda Ballantyne's incomparable volume of amorous advice. Over the course of the series, Esmeralda matches wits (and more) with the resolute Duke of Haynesdale, who is determined to stop her endeavor, no matter the price.

1. The Christmas Conquest

2. The Masquerade of the Marchioness

3. The Widow's Wager

...

~

THE CHRISTMAS CONQUEST

THE LADIES' ESSENTIAL GUIDE TO THE ART OF SEDUCTION #1

PROLOGUE

December 3, 1816—London

*A*lone in her luxurious bed chamber, Esmeralda Ballantyne tilted her mirror to consider the tiny lines at the outer corners of her eyes. They were small and could still be concealed but the day was approaching when that would not be the case.

There was, to her dismay, another silver hair sprouting amongst her raven-black hair. She pulled it out with a savage gesture and peered critically at her reflection again. There could be no mistaking the fact that she grew older—and in her trade, that was no asset. Experience certainly could enhance a courtesan's appeal, but not visible signs of aging.

She stood up from her dressing table with impatience and went to the large mirror, casting her robe aside. Her famously green eyes narrowed as she surveyed herself, taking note of a little extra softness around the belly, a little less lift in the bosom. Stays could disguise a great deal, of course, at least until the bedchamber. Then there could be candlelight. Even so, she would refrain from any sweets or wine for the foreseeable future. She would instruct Nelson to adjust the menu accordingly.

It was a cold and grey day, rain slanting against the windows and a damp permeating the house that no fire could dispel. Worse was the shadow in her heart, which Esmeralda knew was truly at the root of her dissatisfaction.

It was not aging that troubled her so much.

It was a broken heart.

It had been folly of the worst kind for her to fall in love. She knew as much, but she hadn't been able to stop herself once Sebastian Montgomery had stepped into her life. The charm of a handsome man was always enticing but there was something about the Earl of Rockmorton that had intrigued her, a sadness buried beneath his merriment. It had never been her destiny to console him for more than a night or two, but still it gave Esmeralda a pang that he was so happily wed to another. Her mood had been perilously close to despair since the celebration of those nuptials.

She had to find a new path forward.

She would hunt it out this very day.

Esmeralda dressed, as was her habit, and descended to the drawing room to consider her invitations and write her letters. (She chose the new peridot silk gown, a glorious confection that gave her less satisfaction than hoped, a sure sign of her bleak mood.) That room had the largest fireplace in the house and Latimer had set a roaring fire in anticipation of her arrival there. It also had a window that overlooked the street, and her writing table was immediately before it. On many days, it had given her joy to see an arriving gentleman, but on this day—again—Esmeralda did not even look.

The only man she wished to see would never come to her door again. The countess was with child, but even that had only drawn Montgomery closer to his bride. He was well and truly smitten. Worse, Esmeralda actually liked the lady in question. The former Miss Eurydice Goodenham had astonished her several times in a row and was more than a match for Montgomery.

Theirs was that rare breed of marriage that brings out the best in both parties.

Recognizing his happy situation and even being glad of it did nothing, however, to ease the ache in Esmeralda's own heart. That was what made her feel ancient at two-and-thirty. It also diminished her interest in balls, parties, plays and other opportunities to meet noblemen, those with earthy desires and plenty of coin to spend. She had declined an opportunity to become a mistress, not for lack of generous terms but the failure of the man in question to be Montgomery.

That was madness and she knew it well.

This could endure no longer. There were those reliant upon her financial support. Still, she considered the mail with disinterest. More invitations. More plays, more parties, more men. Esmeralda winced, sighed, and began to open them.

What she needed was a diversion. A challenge. She found herself recalling that astonishing interview in which Montgomery's new wife had requested lessons in the amorous arts. Esmeralda had been so astonished that she had complied. Montgomery had found himself an extraordinary bride, to be certain.

It was a pity that she had been compelled to decline the countess' invitation to spend Christmas at Rockmorton Manor. The lady obviously had kindly intentions, but to accept would have been scandalous. A happily wedded couple could not celebrate Christmas with the husband's former mistress! Generosity had clearly overwhelmed good sense.

A carriage drew up to the door as Esmeralda returned to an inspection of her mail. She refused to even glance up, taking refuge in one last moment alone with her thoughts before she had to pretend to be delighted at some man's arrival.

It was unfortunate that she had no other means to make a living than as a courtesan.

"A lady to see you, my lady," Latimer said in his most disapproving tones. "Are you in?"

A lady? Esmeralda spun to see a figure in the foyer wrapped in a voluminous cloak. If Montgomery's new wife intended to disguise her appearance, she had failed. The countess had pushed back the hood and was openly looking at Esmeralda, her expectation clear.

Doubtless Esmeralda's refusal to visit Rockmorton Manor was not going to be accepted.

This was…interesting.

"Of course, Latimer. Please bring tea."

"You cannot decline to come for Christmas," the countess insisted by way of introduction. She perched on the edge of a chair with obvious impatience. She was dressed in a gown of deep blue silk, but neither the dark hue nor the volume of gently gathered silk disguised the ripeness of her belly. She would deliver of the couple's first child in the new year, by Esmeralda's reckoning—but instead of the anticipated stab of jealousy, Esmeralda was glad. She hoped Montgomery would have a son first. She was so busy marveling at her own reaction that she barely heard the countess's next words. "A friend has need of your instruction and I have promised to provide the opportunity for you to help her. She is coming for Christmas and you *must* do so as well."

Instruction? The choice of word was troubling. "I fear I do not understand, my lady."

"My lady," The countess shook her head. "Why do you speak formally to me now? Why have you declined every invitation? I thought we *liked* each other."

"There are social conventions," Esmeralda began gently but her guest waved a hand.

"We must be friends, regardless of those conventions. You, after all, are responsible for my happy situation. Montgomery and I are both so stubborn that we would yet be at odds had it not been for your intervention." She leaned forward and smiled. "You must call me Eurydice."

Esmeralda felt her brows rise. "Surely, you are aware, my lady, that such a relationship would be greatly commented upon."

"I have no care for gossip."

"Perhaps you should."

The younger woman's gaze was steady. "They cannot do me injury. Montgomery's wealth is such that no one will decline him an invitation. Even if they did, my sister, the Duchess of Inverfyre, would rise furiously to my defense." She smiled at the prospect then straightened. "I am resolved to make a difference and you are key to my success."

Esmeralda's smile faded. "I still do not understand."

Eurydice leaned closer. "You told me what was expected of me in the marriage bed."

"I did not. I gave you a book."

Eurydice waved away this objection. "You helped me with an explanation of what no other woman will discuss. My friend is married but I fear that she and her husband do not often meet abed."

"Surely this is a concern between man and wife."

"He spends most of his evenings abroad, seeking entertainment elsewhere." Eurydice straightened. "Not at balls or places where his lady wife would be welcome, either."

"Then it appears that he has no desire to conceive an heir."

Eurydice's lips tightened. "My friend plans to leave

him and return to her father's home in the new year, for she can bear the situation no longer. But she loves him."

"She has told you this?"

"No. Theirs was a practical union, joining her fortune to his title. She never expected love, but I hear it in her voice. And truly, I cannot blame her for losing her heart, given the gentleman in question. It must be set to rights!"

"I fear this situation is not your concern, much less mine."

"You *know* him," Eurydice appealed. "You must know what he likes. You could help Catherine..."

"To?" Esmeralda invited.

Eurydice blushed. "Seduce him, of course." Then she blinked and averted her gaze.

From any other lady, Esmeralda would have doubted her own ears.

In this case, she was intrigued.

"Who is the man in question?" she asked softly.

"Rhys Bettencourt, Baron Trevelaine." Eurydice leaned closer. "They said he was your conquest once."

This time, Esmeralda averted her gaze.

"Is it true?" Eurydice insisted.

"True or not, I will not speak of it." It was strange for Esmeralda to find herself in the position of arguing the side of social convention. She knew Rhys was wed, of course, for the match had been unexpected. She had not seen him in years, herself. "However did you meet the lady?"

"Our husbands are acquaintances. I met them at a house party in September. The men were hunting grouse and Catherine invited me to walk in the rose garden. I suspected she had something to ask me, but she confided in me."

"Indeed," Esmeralda murmured.

"She noted that we were obviously happy together. She confessed that she wanted nothing more than to grant her husband an heir but feared that would never come to be." Eurydice leaned forward. "She wept a little."

"Ah."

"You must understand. She is a most practical woman and not one inclined to emotional displays. I fear she has borne too much."

Esmeralda nodded, her heart touched. She knew Rhys was more than capable of paying the marital debt. Why did he avoid his wife? Was she plain? Was she a shrew? Esmeralda could think of a thousand possibilities, none of which were within her powers to address.

"I knew that I had to help her. She's so lovely and kind, but shy." Eurydice leaned forward. "You have to aid me in this. You simply must."

"I fail to see how that might be done."

"Come for Christmas. They are invited as well. Catherine will have a fortnight to seduce her husband, away from London's temptations. I know she will succeed with your tutelage."

Esmeralda shook her head. "You must see that you cannot invite your husband's former mistress to celebrate Christmas with you. Even Montgomery's wealth will not allow such a faux-pas to be overlooked."

"You must come in disguise," the lady said and Esmeralda blinked. "You will be Sebastian's elderly aunt from the Continent, recently returned, with no one else to visit for the holidays."

A disguise? Esmeralda was intrigued. She had always wondered whether she should have gone on the stage. "She will not take the counsel of an old woman."

"I think she will," Eurydice insisted. "Only you and I and Montgomery will know the truth. Catherine can visit you privately each afternoon for instruction." She took a breath. "I told her that you have buried three husbands and borne seven children."

"Then why do I have no one to visit at Christmas?"

Eurydice dismissed this question. "Because you dislike households bustling with children. Because your sons remind you of their fathers. Because you have not seen Sebastian in years and wish to verify the happiness of your favored nephew. There are any number of plausible explanations. You *must* help her."

Esmeralda found her anticipation rising. "And if I refuse?"

"I will continue to trouble you," Eurydice vowed so calmly that Esmeralda believed her. "I am right and you are more interested than you would like me to realize." The other woman held Esmeralda's gaze, her own eyes filled with conviction.

Latimer cleared his throat and bustled into the room. There were fresh scones which meant that either he or Nelson approved of this unexpected guest.

The two women eyed each other as Latimer delivered the tea tray. "Shall I pour?"

"I will pour, Latimer. Thank you."

Silence reigned as the butler left, quietly closing the door behind himself. Esmeralda poured the tea, thinking furiously. She was already planning how she could disguise herself and what instruction she would give. It was an outrageous suggestion and a highly appealing one. She could enlist the assistance of Ophelia Pearl, an actress she trusted implicitly for reasons best kept secret between the two of them. Ophelia could help with her disguise, and could herself pretend to be a lady's maid.

"I will send the carriage for you," Eurydice said. "If that is your concern."

"No," Esmeralda said. "You cannot send a carriage here. I will arrive at your London house in a cab the day before you plan to leave London, then travel to Rockmorton Manor with you. That is what an elderly aunt would do. She would not undertake such a journey alone. And I will bring a maid, one who will aid in my disguise."

Eurydice's eyes lit. "Then you will do it?"

"I will accept your challenge," Esmeralda agreed, then smiled that her guest's delight was so clear.

"I won't tell Catherine in advance. She might cancel if she knew our plan."

Esmeralda raised a brow that it was now 'our' plan.

"You must tell her about your aunt."

"Oh, I already have. She doesn't know that her husband has been invited. He wished for his presence to be a surprise, which gives me hope for their future."

Esmeralda nodded. That would be Rhys. He had always been one of the most honorable men she had known. Again, she wondered what had gone awry between the pair.

Here was the challenge she had sought, and for a good cause!

Her guest accepted a scone and sipped her tea, evidently content to let her hostess consider the details and plan.

"There will be no afternoon tutelage," Esmeralda said finally. "I could be identified as the source of information too readily. No, I must conceive of a more subtle way to offer instruction."

"I trust that you will do as much." The countess looked so hopeful that Esmeralda nodded reassurance.

"I wonder which of us will enjoy this challenge the most."

"It should be Catherine."

"If not Rhys."

The two laughed together lightly, and Esmeralda felt a new bond with Montgomery's wife.

"The only possible concern is Catherine's benefactor," Eurydice noted.

What a curious choice of words.

"Benefactor?" Esmeralda echoed.

"What else should I call him? He arranged the match, you know."

Esmeralda felt her eyes narrow. "I do *not* know," she said quietly, but a memory stirred of some gossip overheard. So many rumors and so many lies, tangled around so many secrets and truths. She had never been able to keep them straight, let alone recall them all.

"Gaming debts," Eurydice confided in a whisper. "The baron owed Damien DeVries, the Duke of Haynesdale, and could not pay."

Esmeralda's heart skipped a beat. On her arrival in London, she had believed Damien DeVries to be the most wickedly handsome man alive—with the daredevil nature to match. The third and youngest son of the Duke of Haynesdale and unlikely to inherit, he had been a young and reckless rebel who had fascinated Esmeralda. Then his father had bought him a commission and she had not seen him again. He had been wounded, if she recalled correctly, and had become a recluse after inheriting the title, against those long odds.

They said his luck had held, but she doubted he saw the matter in that light.

"The match was arranged as a result," the countess concluded.

"Your friend is wealthy, then?"

"Her father and uncle are the publishers, Carruthers & Carruthers."

Rhys had a common wife, whose fortune came from trade. That was certainly one reason why he might avoid his bride's bed.

Eurydice continued. "I have never met the duke, but they say he was a handsome man before his injuries. If he forbade their visit, Catherine would heed his injunction without hesitation."

'Handsome' did not begin to describe the charms of the Duke of Haynesdale, in Esmeralda's view. The man was the most glorious specimen of masculinity she had ever seen. He was brilliant as well as an accomplished sportsman, and fiendishly accurate when he dueled. It was more than luck that guided his hand. She felt a flutter of a different kind of anticipation at even the distant prospect of encountering him again. Unlike many others, Esmeralda thought scars added to a man's allure. "He was quite handsome, as I recall," she contented herself with saying, then changed the subject. "Tell me what details of this scheme have been decided."

"We leave for Cornwall a week tomorrow, on the tenth."

"I will arrive at your house in Berkley Square the afternoon before, though you might not recognize me."

"Oh! What will your name be?"

Esmeralda considered this. "Mrs. Delilah Oliver."

"Let us precisely define your relation to my husband."

"An excellent notion." The two women leaned closer, dropping their voices as they conferred about details. By the time the teapot was empty, they had established Delilah's tale in detail.

After Eurydice's departure, Esmeralda stared into the fire, marvelling at this opportunity. What if it was only the first such chance? What if there were legions of women who had no notion how to seduce their husbands? She recalled all the men who had complained about their wives' skills—or lack thereof—in the bedroom, but she knew as well as Eurydice that there was no reputable way for a woman to learn such arts. Married as a maiden, given only the barest warning by a mother or nursemaid, a new bride was reliant upon her husband to offer instruction in the art of pleasure. Esmeralda knew many did not. To redress that imbalance was a most tantalizing prospect.

First, she had to succeed with Catherine and Rhys, as well as perfect her disguise as Delilah Oliver. And there was precious little time! She had only a week to arrange all. She refused to spend one more moment recalling the Duke of Haynesdale. If all went well, their paths would never cross.

Which was a pity, to be sure.

LITTLE DID Esmeralda realize that when her butler and cook conferred in the kitchen over their late-morning cup of tea, Latimer informed Nelson that the lady's spirits rose again. "She has that old glint in her eyes again," he said with satisfaction. "Like she has made a wager with the Devil himself. I knew she would rise to the challenge again, Doris. Did I not say as much?"

"That you did, Bert. That you did."

"You were right about that lady calling."

"I had a feeling. It was the scones as made all come aright."

"I would wager upon that, Doris. There is no one makes a scone as well as you do."

"You just want another," Nelson teased. When he laughed, she served him another, then poured him a fresh cup of hot black tea.

"She has given me a most uncommon list of items to procure," Latimer admitted as he bit into his scone.

"That's our lady," Nelson said with approval. "Always with a little mystery in the works." The pair, a widow and a widower well content with their position and inordinately fond of their mistress, toasted each other with their tea and each had another scone in celebration.

~

AT THE SAME MOMENT, Rhys Bettencourt, Baron Trevelaine, waited with some impatience for his solicitor, Mr. Murdoch of Murdoch, Murdoch & Fitch, to make his point. He was well accustomed to Mr. Murdoch's apparent inability to confide any detail in a hurry, but Rhys had been irked before he arrived.

Apparently, his wife had decided to spend Christmas elsewhere, instead of at either his London house or country estate—or with Rhys. She was not even visiting her own family, but would be staying with a friend.

At Rockmorton Manor in Cornwall.

Worse, he had learned of her plans from his valet, who had heard Catherine's maid discussing the journey. Rhys knew that they did not interact often, but it was *Christmas*. And Catherine was the closest to family he had.

Though that, his solicitor would undoubtedly have noted if given the chance, was Rhys' own fault.

Mr. Murdoch cleared his throat and continued. "It is, you must understand, my lord, a matter of some delicacy, and one upon which I am not entirely privy to detail, but it was my conviction that you should be aware…"

"Do tell me, Mr. Murdoch," Rhys said. "I believe I can bear whatever tidings you would like to share."

"Very well. The matter concerns your wife, sir."

Rhys straightened at this mention of Catherine. "Is she ill?" he asked immediately, though there was no reason his solicitor should know more than himself if that were the case. Mr. Murdoch must have come to the same conclusion for his expression became stern. "I meant, has she discovered any additional plague upon the books of my estates?"

It was not a graceful correction but Mr. Murdoch simply shook his head. He frowned and removed his pince-nez. "I encountered her father yesterday, quite by chance, and he made a most curious comment."

Again the older man paused.

"Indeed?" Rhys invited.

"Mr. Carruthers said he would be relieved to see his daughter happy again in the new year. I assumed that the lady was with child and the tidings would be shared then, but it quickly became clear that we spoke of different situations. It was rather embarrassing for both of us." Mr. Murdoch replaced his pince-nez and glared through them at Rhys. "Mr. Carruthers explained that he has invited his daughter to return to live at his home. He said no more upon the matter, for he is the soul of discretion."

Rhys hid his dismay with a terse comment. "It seems not if he confided that much in you in a chance encounter."

"I believe, my lord, that he is a kindly father, much concerned with the happiness of his daughters." His gaze fixed upon Rhys expectantly. "I can only hope his impression is untrue."

"My wife and I meet monthly to review the books, Mr. Murdoch. Otherwise, we each go our own way quite contentedly." Even to Rhys, it sounded like a tepid marital situation—and truly, he was not content with the situation. Catherine seemed to be.

"Is your wife with child?"

Rhys averted his gaze. He would not have tolerated such a blunt question from a stranger, but he had known Mr. Murdoch all his life and the man had been a great confidante of his own father. "I do not believe so."

In fact, he knew she was not. She could not be.

Mr. Murdoch exhaled. "If Mr. Carruthers is correct, you must recognize the possible repercussions of such a decision."

"Why would she accept such an invitation?" Rhys asked with impatience. "My wife has the run of the London house, while I spend most of my time in the country. When I am in town, we scarcely see each other, save for our monthly meetings."

Mr. Murdoch shook his head. "And it does not occur to you that this may be the cause of any unhappiness on her part?"

"Our choices of entertainment are at variance, Mr. Murdoch. My wife has no interest in cards or society or even the theatre. She has all the books she could desire, and more besides."

"That is not, in my experience, sir, the reason ladies wed." Mr. Murdoch's tone was as dry as a desert.

Rhys straightened and spoke with just as much asperity. "We wed, if you recall, Mr. Murdoch, because the Duke of Haynesdale arranged the match and insisted upon it. I had no choice and the lady was not unwilling, but neither of us had particularly high expectations."

The solicitor was stern. "The match saw your debts paid, my lord, and a daughter past her prime years agreeably settled with a husband and title. It seemed a most suitable solution."

"Especially given the pledge demanded by my father on his deathbed."

"If I may be so bold, my lord, that request was unreasonable upon his part."

"But he was correct, as subsequent events proved."

The two men's gazes locked over the wide wooden expanse of Mr. Murdoch's desk.

The older man finally shook his head and considered the documents before him. "If the baroness departs your household, it is unlikely that she will request a divorce and out of the question that she will demand an annulment."

Mr. Murdoch did not look up at that point, or he might have noted a change in Rhys' expression. Fortunately, the solicitor did not know that the marriage remained unconsummated. Was this invitation the reason why Catherine would be away at Christmas?

Would she actually leave his house? The prospect was troubling. Rhys relied upon Catherine's good sense and practicality, and he admired how she managed his household so adeptly. He liked knowing she was there and though she did not know it, he always paused outside her chamber door when he returned at night, listening to her sleep. The sound of her voice, even at a distance, always made him smile.

Making her smile always counted as one of the great triumphs of his day.

"The Duke of Haynesdale will undoubtedly be displeased," Mr. Murdoch continued. "For he is not a man to appreciate the failure of one of his schemes."

"I'm not afraid of Haynesdale."

"You are the one who has lost to him before." Mr. Murdoch harrumphed. "The greater concern is financial, I must say. I doubt that the dowry brought to the marriage by your lady wife could be retrieved, except in the case of an annulment which cannot occur, but her father is a prudent man. Those investments responsible for her annual income, which has become part of your income, are being transferred from Mr. Carruthers to you in stages, if you recall, so concerned was he in ensuring that his daughter was not snared in a mercenary match."

Rhys remembered the sting of Mr. Carruthers' suspicion. "And if the transfers were halted?"

Mr. Murdoch consulted a document and pursed his lips. "You would have to sell at least one house and probably half of the horses. Even in the remaining house, staff would have to be reduced, as well as your own spending."

His solicitor did not fail to mince words, once he finally began.

"I daresay it would be tactless, given the situation, to ask your lady wife about the specific impact, but the baroness does have an admirably clear head for figures." Mr. Murdoch shook his head in apparent wonder. "It is a most remarkable trait in a young woman."

Clearly, Rhys' situation was dire and it was time to put aside his scruples.

Mr. Murdoch shuffled his papers, the image of a man with more to say.

"I suppose you have advice for me, Mr. Murdoch."

"I can only conclude, sir, that it would be an excellent time to see your lady wife in the family way. You might spend an agreeable Christmas together, somewhere quiet, and ensure that matter is resolved. You could have an heir by next Christmas and she would have every reason to remain comfortably at Trevelaine House." Mr. Murdoch gave him a hard look. "Consider that a mother is never anxious to abandon her child."

The advice was practical and yet sounded predatory to Rhys. He liked Catherine too much to take advantage of her. On the other hand, their marriage had been thus from the start: her fortune and his title, and little else to bind them together beyond a vow. Rhys was not a man inclined to meddle when all proceeded according to plan, and all had proceeded extremely well since Catherine had taken his accounts in hand.

He had come to rely upon the wife he had not even wanted.

It appeared that the time had come for a change to

their established rhythm, though. He pondered his limited options as Mr. Murdoch summarized and reviewed what he had already confided, then Rhys took his leave.

Why the deuce was Catherine going to Rockmorton Manor in Cornwall for Christmas?

Fortunately, he knew precisely where to find Sebastian Montgomery, Earl of Rockmorton, at this hour of a Thursday afternoon. Once he would have sought his friend at Brooke's, but marriage had tempered Montgomery's inclinations.

"White's," Rhys instructed his driver as he stepped into his waiting carriage. Was it even possible for him to seduce his dispassionate and practical wife? He was quite certain she disapproved of him and he doubted she would welcome physical pleasure.

It appeared that this Christmas, however, Rhys must find out.

CHAPTER 1

December 20, 1816—Rockmorton Manor, Cornwall

There was no evading the fact that Rhys Bettencourt was utterly indifferent to his wife. He had left his London house for his country estate for Christmas without sparing the lady in question a word of farewell.

Catherine Bettencourt née Carruthers, the wife in question, wished she might have felt the same way about her handsome rake of a husband. Rhys was everything she was not: impulsive, reckless and devastatingly charming, at ease in every situation and confident before every challenge. She was incredulous that Rhys had wed her at all, but the Duke of Haynesdale was not a man to be put aside.

Even the duke, with all his influence, could not force a marriage to be happy. Catherine and her husband lived in the same house, save when he went to the country. Either way, they saw each other only once a month, for the review of the accounts. It was pathetic how Catherine looked forward to those meetings, which her husband must just endure. Her management of the accounts was the one thing she contributed to his household, but Catherine would not have been a woman if she had not wished to be more than *useful*.

And now he took himself off for Christmas. What man would want to be reminded of the plain blue-stocking he had been compelled to wed? Not Baron Trevelaine! Doubtless, he had invited all his cronies to Trevelaine Manor, to hunt and shoot and gorge themselves. Catherine might return in the new year to discover that he had filled the London house with doxies and Cyprians, established a gaming hell in the drawing room, and emptied the wine cellar for his guests. Her absence would scarce be noted.

Her presence was certainly not desired. She did not play cards. She disliked gambling and had no interest in gossip; she did not worry overmuch about clothes or gems. She adored books, plain and simple, and invariably was in the midst of reading several. Catherine was dull, by society definitions, and worse, she watched her husband's finances closely. He was not going to fritter away her fortune as he had done his own, not while she was present to intervene.

Perhaps that made her a shrew.

Perhaps that gave Rhys another reason to avoid her.

Catherine read the same paragraph in the same book for the hundredth time and did not manage to comprehend it. The book, after all, had nothing to do with Baron Trevelaine and his current pursuits, the sole subject that occupied her thoughts in this moment.

She frowned and began the passage again.

"Is it a good book, my lady?"

"I fear not," Catherine admitted.

"Is it ripe with salacious detail?" Foster asked, in a highly accurate mimicry of Catherine's father.

Despite the impudence, Catherine could not entirely suppress her smile. "No. Perhaps it would be better if it was."

Foster laughed and Catherine removed her glasses to consider the maid seated opposite her in the carriage. Lucy Foster was young but consistently cheerful, as well as quite pretty with her thickly lashed blue eyes and raven-dark hair. It was impossible to be vexed with Foster for long and Catherine was glad once again that the girl had accompanied her to Trevelaine.

"You know you are impertinent," Catherine chided gently.

Foster smiled, unrepentant. "If I may say as much, my lady, one of the things I like best about being in your service is that you allow some blunt speech in private."

It was true. Catherine had always allowed her maids to speak freely when they were alone together.

"I like that you are so merry, Foster," Catherine replied in kind. "It does a soul good to know that one person in her circle will smile each day."

Foster grinned at the praise. "I could not do otherwise, my lady. You and your family have always been so good to me. I only hope that I give satisfaction."

"You do, Foster." Catherine returned to the book manuscript she had agreed to read for her father. The brothers and partners of Carruthers & Carruthers had found success in their most recent publishing venture, contracting novels for publication and supply to circulating libraries. Neither Catherine's father nor uncle, however, considered themselves capable of deciding which books would best satisfy their growing list of clients, so Catherine read the manuscripts, sorting those with potential from those that had none. In truth, she was glad to have such a satisfactory means of filling her time.

This one was abysmal. She placed it in the one satchel on the floor of the carriage that already contained half a dozen manuscripts, and chose another from the satchel of contenders. A brief glance out the window revealed that the rain continued to fall in torrents. She opened the book.

"It is unfortunate that his lordship could not accompany us," Foster said with a wistful sigh. She was not alone among the female servants of the household in having a *tendre* for the baron.

"My lord husband wished to spend Christmas at Trevelaine Manor." In truth, he had said no such thing. Catherine had not even had the opportunity to tell him of her plans before he had left.

She would not feel guilty about that.

"But to be alone at Christmas!"

"He will hardly be alone, Foster. Trevelaine Manor is undoubtedly filled to the rafters by now with his friends." Catherine knew she sounded tart, but visions of the inevitable celebration in her absence haunted her.

She would not even think of the bills. Her husband likely would not.

"How long until we reach Rockmorton Manor?" Foster asked moments later. "I feel it has been *years* since we left London."

"Fielding said it would be early this afternoon," she said, referring to the driver. "It might be shortly, now." She frowned and read, feigning indifference as well as she could.

Foster fidgeted, turning from one window to the other, then fixed her attention upon Catherine again. "Is Rockmorton Manor a large house, do you think, my lady?"

"I have no information."

"I hope the servants are not unkind to newcomers," the maid confessed quietly. "In some houses, they can be beastly, I hear."

"I cannot imagine that Lady Montgomery would tolerate as much."

"That is true. I do miss Carruthers House in that way, my lady. We had such jolly times in the kitchen. And Mr. Wentworth always read aloud to us on Saturday nights." Foster sighed in reminiscence. "I did like that."

"I thought you liked Trevelaine House."

"They are more friendly to me now than was once the case, to be sure, my lady. They do not have so much to say about you, my lady, at least not before me." Foster hurried on, and Catherine guessed there had been comments about the source of her family's wealth. It was hard-earned, every penny of it! "And it is a grand house, so grand that I do not have to share my chamber. That stands in its favor. But no one reads to us. It makes the evenings most long." She sighed again.

Catherine did not know what to say to that, so she struggled to read.

She heard Fielding call to the horses long moments later and the carriage slowed. Foster peeked out the window, her excitement obvious. "Oh, it is lovely, even in the rain! I've never been to Cornwall, my lady. Is that the sea?"

"It must be, though I have never been here either." Catherine packed away her books and tucked her glasses into her reticule. Her vision was excellent for distance but not for reading or needlework. She fastened her blue wool coat again while Foster artfully arranged the ribbons of her bonnet. The girl had a touch with bows and fripperies that Catherine could not begin to emulate. She then tugged on her dark blue leather gloves and squared her shoulders, as prepared as possible to greet her host and hostess.

She knew Eurydice. There was no cause for consternation. But Catherine had never been at ease among strangers and she gripped her hands together in her lap, fretting about the inevitable exchanges. It would be fine.

The rain pattered to a halt on the roof and the sun peeked out from behind the clouds. That made her think of Rhys, who had the most remarkable good fortune with the weather. Even the sun, it seemed, could not resist that man, for it shone upon him without fail.

Foster's eyes danced with excitement. The younger woman leaned forward to peek out the window when Fielding hailed someone. Was that Lord Montgomery who called a greeting? It had sounded almost like Rhys...Catherine's heart sank, even as she chided herself for being foolish.

"Oh!" Foster said with delight.

Catherine looked out the window to see the familiar silhouette of her husband striding closer. He wore his tall black boots, polished to a gleam, buff breeches and a jacket of deepest green. His cravat was knotted with flair and secured with the emerald pin he favored. His top hat was buffed to a sheen. His greatcoat hung open, flaring behind him as he walked, and she saw his teeth flash as he laughed at some comment made by Fielding. He was the most handsome man alive, she was certain of it. Catherine was as awed by him as if they had never met and felt her throat tighten in trepidation.

Her husband had auburn hair that he wore a bit long so that it curled over his collar, and his eyes were sparkling green. He had the aquiline nose of a Roman emperor and features so chiseled that he might have been a god. There was a cleft in his chin and invariably a glint of mischief danced in his eyes. His charm was legendary and his conquests beyond reckoning. He had a reputation as a rake, though he had always treated Catherine with such courtesy that she might have been his sister—perhaps he had guessed that no effort on his behalf was required for her to be dazzled.

His very presence turned her to a stammering, incoherent fool.

How could he even be at Rockmorton Manor?

And why?

Rhys removed his hat as he opened the door, then offered a gloved hand to Catherine, as smoothly assured as ever. In contrast, her very innards quivered—and the man had not even met her gaze. The sunlight burnished his hair to copper and lingered lovingly on his broad shoulders.

"My lady," he said in that low rumble of a voice that gave Catherine palpitations. His gaze rose to meet hers and her heart stopped cold. She could feel a blush beginning to rise over her chest and it seemed she had forgotten how to utter a sound.

There was no ignoring the wickedness in his eyes and she knew he savored her surprise. Catherine felt her lips set, impatient with both her reaction and his apparent need to tease her like a child. "Sir," she managed to say.

"I trust you had a comfortable journey?" he asked gallantly. "The hours have been long awaiting your arrival."

What nonsense! Foster gave a minute sigh of appreciation that Catherine ignored. Catherine put her hand in that of her husband and concentrated on alighting from the carriage without stumbling. "Forgive my astonishment, sir. I did not expect to encounter you in Cornwall." Her words sounded tight and formal, even to herself, but it took all within her to address him directly.

"Do I detect disappointment, my lady?" he asked in a whisper. "Did you think to be spared my company at

Christmas?" His tone was teasing but there was a hard current beneath his words.

Catherine's cheeks burned that she had been caught. "Surprise, sir," she admitted. "Indeed, I marvel at your presence here." She dared to glance up only to find that he was still watching her. His gaze was intent, his eyes dark and unfathomable, the line of his lips grim. Her flush burned like fire, for she hated that Eurydice and Montgomery were watching this encounter. "I was certain you were merry at Trevelaine Manor."

Rhys lowered his head to murmur in her ear. "Would you believe me if I said I could not bear to celebrate the Yule without you?" The fan of his breath gave her shivers.

Catherine saw no reason to lie "No, sir, I would not." She saw his eyes narrow. Did he expect her to enjoy his jest at her expense? As ever, anger gave a fluidity to her speech, overcoming her reaction to his presence. "It would be irrational for you to undertake such an effort to see me now when you could have readily done so with little exertion the better part of these last two years." Yet again, she sounded formal and forbidding.

Indeed, the man fairly flinched—though her words were true enough—and Catherine wished she had kept silent.

"You should have spoken to me of your intention."

"I left you a note upon my departure, sir."

"You might have spoken to me directly."

"You had already departed, sir, for Trevelaine Manor."

"No, no, Catherine," he chided softly. "You had decided before that."

She looked at him, feeling the blood drain from her face. How did he know?

He leaned down to whisper to her, his grip firm on

her hand and his gaze unswerving. "I left for Rock-morton Manor because I had learned it was your desti-nation. The sole question is why?" One brow lifted, inviting her confession. "Is something awry in our household? Are you unhappy?"

Catherine could not utter a word. So snared was she by his attention that her mouth opened and closed in silence.

She was no better than a fish, she thought crossly.

"I desired a change, sir, no more than that."

"Perhaps you plan an assignation," he murmured wickedly.

Catherine gasped in outrage, cheeks burning hot as she recovered her tongue. "That suggestion, sir, is un-warranted, unkind and utterly unjustified. I have given you no cause for such a heinous suspicion and I cannot believe that even you would think…"

She fell silent when Rhys flicked a gloved fingertip across her cheek. "It is a welcome sight to see you an-noyed with me again, Catherine. I should have pro-voked you sooner."

"That would have been unkind, sir." Vexing man! He looked to be utterly pleased with himself—while she was flustered and disheveled by his manner and his presence, and unable to think of a reasonable thing to say.

Let alone a charming one.

She would have turned to meet their host and host-ess, but Rhys lifted her hand to his lips, his gaze locked with hers. His eyes were impossibly dark and he ap-peared to be more serious than she had ever seen him. Catherine could only stare, transfixed. "On the con-trary, my lady, I am beguiled by any hint that an un-tamed fire burns within your heart. Thus far, only the disorder of my accounts has ignited your outrage." That brow rose again, inviting her to remember.

Catherine would never forget that exchange. "I had never seen such wasteful habits, sir, or such a wanton and profligate dispersal of coin…"

"So you have said." Rhys smiled and pressed a kiss to her fingers. "Imagine what might spark if that flame was fanned." His eyes fairly glowed and Catherine could not draw a breath.

"You would scandalize me, sir."

"On the contrary, I would seduce you."

Seduce her?

Why, after two years of marriage, would Rhys suddenly turn his attention upon her? She did not deceive herself that this man cared a whit for her, or even for a scandal. His presence in Cornwall and his expenditure of charm was incomprehensible.

If flattering. Oh, it was a marvel to be the focus of his attention and his gaze made her warm to her toes. It muddled her thoughts and made it impossible for her to discern his motives.

She had to put distance between them, at once, the better to solve this riddle.

"It is unseemly for us to confer in private while our host and hostess await us." She tried to pull her hand away but Rhys held fast and placed it on his elbow. He covered it with his own hand, keeping her fingers trapped there.

"No need to start rumors, my lady," he murmured silkily.

"I always understood you had no care for idle gossip."

"I do not, but I believe that you do." He turned that piercing gaze upon her and Catherine's mouth went dry. He studied her so intently, as if she was the mysterious one, that she was struck dumb. Again. "I witnessed your parting from Mrs. Grieves at Trevelaine Manor a year ago, after all."

Catherine dropped her gaze to the ground as her cheeks burned in recollection of that unwelcome exchange. "I confess I have forgotten what she said," she managed after a silence that stretched to eternity.

Rhys laughed lightly. "Oh, my lady, you are a poor liar."

"I...I..." Catherine found herself once again blushing furiously.

"And I am glad," Rhys whispered, his breath against her ear. "I think you would have to be dead to forget her broad hint that she expected to see an heir by this Yule. I cannot blame you for avoiding another such exchange, or another gift of her family cure for infertility. A sensible woman like yourself would see no reason to spend Christmas at Trevelaine Manor."

Catherine could not believe they were discussing a matter of such intimacy while walking toward their waiting host and hostess. "She meant well," she managed to say.

"That would be her tale, to be sure. You probably do not realize that I reprimanded her."

Catherine stopped to look up at him in surprise. "You did? But Mrs. Grieves has been with your family since before you were born."

"Then she should have known better than to be so familiar with my wife." There was a steely glint in Rhys' eyes that made Catherine's heart skip. "I considered asking her to leave my employ, but Henderson intervened on her behalf."

Was it true? Catherine wanted so much to believe him that she feared she was gullible.

"Henderson, you should know, insisted that you would be distressed if anyone were dismissed for an inappropriate word." Rhys' lips thinned. "I ceded to him in the hope that he was right."

Henderson was hardly her champion, Catherine

knew. Trevelaine's butler had been most critical of her origins, yet he evidently understood her all the same.

How remarkable.

"I did not think you ever reprimanded anyone, sir."

Her husband's smile was slow and utterly beguiling. "It is a new skill of mine, learned these past two years from example."

"I do not understand."

He leaned closer, eyes gleaming. "No one ever reprimanded me before you, my lady."

"Then that explains your dislike of me."

"Dislike?" Rhys appeared to be surprised. "On the contrary, I think there is merit in having someone in one's life who will utter the truth when it is of import." His gaze warmed, against every expectation, then his eyes began to twinkle again. "It was both deserved and duly noted. Have I not reformed my ways?"

Her cheeks were burning with the awareness that she should never have chastised him over his expenses, but she had been outraged at the time. "You have, sir." It was true. She could find no fault with his spending now.

"Then you might be interested to learn that you are not alone in finding fault. Just this very month, I have been taken to task by the honorable Mr. Murdoch over my failure to conceive an heir with any punctuality. It seems that in his view, I am ignoring my responsibilities to both you and my title." Before she could decide what to make of that, Rhys swept off his hat and bowed before her. "And now you know, my lady wife, why I am at Rockmorton Manor. I come to mend my wicked ways."

Catherine was skeptical and feared it showed, for her husband smiled wolfishly.

Then he leaned astonishingly close, so close that she could smell the heat of his skin. She stiffened at the feel of his lips beside her ear and delicious shivers slid over her skin. She was almost in his arms and closed her eyes, realizing how much she yearned for that very thing. "As promised, I am here to seduce you thoroughly, my lady wife, upon my solicitor's orders."

Catherine's thoughts froze then her annoyance rose. She was not a romantic, but her husband could have let her believe his appearance was his own idea, rather than an injunction from his solicitor.

He kissed her temple, the fleeting touch of his lips against her skin sending a tide of heat to her toes, and stepped back. Those eyes danced merrily and his lips tugged into a slight smile, so assured was he of his success.

So confident was he that she had been simply waiting for his attention to alight upon her.

Anger flared again.

It was the money. Rhys was here, at his solicitor's behest, because somehow he had learned of her father's suggestion that she return to his house. Rhys had come to guarantee his access to her annual income. She was useful and she was rich, and beyond that, she held no merit for him. The truth was bitter, though just two years before she had expected no more.

"I see," Catherine said, managing to speak calmly as if her entire person was not in tumult. "How enlightening to know just what inducement is required for you to expend any of your attention upon *me*. I suppose I must write and thank Mr. Murdoch." She then looked her husband in the eye. "Shall I also thank him for sharing my plans for the new year?"

Rhys sobered. "Catherine, you cannot return to your father's house. We are *wed*."

"That does not mean we must abide together, sir." she said, her words fluid in disappointment. She was right and oh, she did not want to be. She spoke crisply.

"Society is filled with couples who live hundreds of miles from each other quite happily. I see no reason why we should continue a charade for the sake of appearances that concern neither of us."

Dismay flashed in Rhys' eyes. "I will change your mind..." he began in a growl.

"Not with your intended seduction," she replied, then turned and strode toward their host and hostess, chin high. When he spoke thus, she could forget her own name. The man had a fearsome power over her, even when he did not try to arouse her. What would it be like to have Rhys truly intent on seducing her? The very notion made Catherine dizzy.

"No, it is only the matter of money that claims your passion," Rhys muttered behind her and she almost pivoted in her astonishment.

Could he believe she did not welcome his attentions?

Catherine blinked and continued, fighting her emotional turmoil. The advanced state of Eurydice's pregnancy prompted a stab of envy that nearly took her to her knees, but she hid that reaction along with all others.

Why was her husband the one man who could so confound her? She had not expected love in her marriage, but neither had she anticipated that she would be the only one to succumb to Cupid's arrow. She had been a fool to enjoy those afternoons in the library conferring over the books of his estates, imagining that they established common ground and built a future together.

His sole interest in her was her fortune.

Catherine blinked back tears that had no reason to rise and forced a smile for her hostess.

"Lady Montgomery!" she said. "How radiant you look!"

CATHERINE HAD DONE IT AGAIN.

Just when Rhys reconciled himself to the cause of the greater good, Catherine's fury brought her to life. She might have been mistaken for a statue most of the time, for she was the very image of composure. With her fair skin and blond hair, her pallor could have been mistaken for stone, especially as she inclined to silence. She could be as easily overlooked as a stone pillar. But when she was angry, Catherine's demeanor changed completely. Her eyes flashed blue fire, her cheeks flushed, and she was smoothly articulate, intelligence echoing in her every syllable. She fascinated him when she turned to goddess of fire and fury.

She had first made the transformation on the day after their wedding.

Rhys had not sought out the lady before the wedding ceremony, so disgruntled was he to be forced into a match arranged by the Duke of Haynesdale, and worse a marriage to a maiden of twenty-five—on the shelf—whose rich dowry had been earned in trade. The daughter of a publisher, the unknown lady's lack of aristocratic birth had rankled.

He had met his bride at the altar and been utterly underwhelmed by her appearance. Catherine was said to be plain, so he had been prepared for that, but he had not expected her tongue-tied silence or refusal to meet his gaze. Little had he guessed that she could be a tempest when roused, as she had been by the next morning.

Left to her own devices when he went to his club, she had requested the accounts to his holdings and spent the remainder of their wedding day reviewing them. The next morning, she chastised him for his wasteful habits. She was so glorious when enraged that Rhys had only been able to stare in wonder. The statue had come to life, eyes flashing and cheeks flushed, so splendidly coherent in her condemnations that she could argue in the House of Lords. He was thunderstruck by her fury and her beauty.

If Catherine had guessed that he had nearly taken her on that worn leather couch that day, she would never have spoken to him again.

What stopped him was the family curse, for he was not prepared to lose her—even for their mutual satisfaction.

As a result, they might as well have been siblings these past two years. They spoke politely to each other. They ate the occasional meal together. They conferred each month over questions of the household. She read incessantly, perhaps to evade his company. His house had become filled with books, but he could not complain about the expense since most were borrowed from her father's business.

She would leave him soon unless he changed her mind.

Rhys knew it was not Murdoch's instruction that fed his desire to charm his bride now. He strode after the lady and claimed her elbow anew, ignoring how she stiffened slightly at his touch.

Her reaction rankled. He was not precisely an ogre.

"Catherine! I am delighted to see you again," Lady Montgomery declared. She was wearing a cloak with a heavy fur collar and holding her husband's arm, as if she might be unsteady upon her feet. Rhys could not look at her ripe belly, for he needed no reminder of the peril in this lady's future. "You cannot imagine how many books I have gathered to lend to you."

"The house lists ever so slightly now," Montgomery said solemnly. "The library floor having a disproportionate weight to bear."

Catherine turned a smile upon Montgomery that

Rhys thought undeserved. "It was so kind of you to invite us."

"Do not be deceived. My lady wife covets your books," Montgomery whispered with a mischievous wink. "The countess has her own dark scheme."

The lady in question gave him a playful nudge. "We are agreed that there is nothing so satisfying as a good book," she retorted. "That is what I like about Catherine. She loves books as much as I do."

"I find that difficult to believe," Rhys said lightly from behind Catherine and felt her start a little. "My wife's passion for books is unexcelled in my experience."

"Then we shall have a most excellent time," Lady Montgomery said. "I shall have to challenge your ascendancy."

"It will not be easy for our guest to best you in this matter," Montgomery teased. "Perhaps Bettencourt and I should research the possibilities of extending the libraries at our respective homes." He then directed Rhys' attention to the clear view of the village in the distance and the sea beyond.

"Come out of the wind," their hostess urged Catherine. "It is so bitter today. I have had a fire set in your chamber already, in case the carriage was cold."

"It was chilly," Catherine agreed, stepping away from Rhys as if it did not trouble her to do as much. He did not share her indifference and could not tear his gaze from her until she vanished into the house.

She did not even glance back.

He became aware of Montgomery's gaze upon him and smiled for his host. "Were you not going to show me that new gelding in your stables today?"

CHAPTER 2

Rockmorton Manor was a lovely home of admirable proportions and welcoming manner. The foyer of the house was graced with a large fireplace, and there was a blazing fire upon the hearth. The mantle had been decked in greenery and there were greens wound through the spindles on the great curving staircase. Red ribbons had been tied at intervals in the garland and the house smelled pleasantly of pine and roasted meat. There was even a cluster of mistletoe hanging from the pendant in the foyer, but Catherine did not let her gaze linger upon it.

Did Rhys believe she did not desire him? It was absurd, given his qualities, but Catherine had to admit that she was either silent in his presence, concerned with the accounts, or angry.

What if her comparative solitude was her own fault?

"The house is lovely," she said to Eurydice with a smile. "It looks so festive for the season."

"I am convinced it is the best place to be at Christmas." Her hostess smiled. "You will adore the library."

"I am certain I shall."

"I have left a few books in your chamber that I have enjoyed recently."

Catherine could only feel anticipation for she knew that Eurydice shared her taste in fiction. "I thank you. I have brought many book manuscripts at the behest of my father. I would welcome your opinion on the more promising ones."

"I should love to read them! How exciting it must be to discover a book that no one yet has read." Eurydice caught her breath at the base of the stairs and unfastened her cloak, making the advanced state of her pregnancy more evident. What would Catherine give to share that state? What of her pride? "May I take your arm for the stairs?" Eurydice asked. "I do become winded rather quickly these days."

"Of course. We shall take it slowly."

"I take everything slowly these days," Eurydice acknowledged with a laugh. "But I must show you to your room. I hope you will like it."

"I am certain that I will."

Eurydice paused halfway up the stairs, visibly catching her breath. She smiled at Catherine. "Am I mistaken that you were surprised to find Bettencourt here?"

"I was and am. He gave no indication of his intentions."

"You must be pleased," her hostess whispered, her eyes shining. "I cannot think of a single lady who would be dismayed by the prospect of his attention."

Catherine chose her words with care. There was no cause to evade the truth. "I know I am not the kind of woman who might claim his heart."

"You might be surprised." Eurydice's smile turned impish. "What if you could do as much?"

"That would be wondrous," Catherine admitted, though she doubted it could be done.

There was a maid in the upstairs corridor and Eurydice's tone became less confidential. "I apologize that

Mrs. Oliver, Montgomery's aunt, is not present to greet you. She tends to nap in the afternoon and I did not wish to wake her. Bettencourt has not even met her as yet. She found the journey from London most tiring and has been keeping to her chamber. I hope she comes down for dinner tonight."

Catherine had not been aware that her host had an aunt or another guest, but it seemed most reasonable for family to gather this time of year. "I am content to make her acquaintance at her convenience."

"I knew you would understand." At the end of the corridor were two closed doors. Eurydice halted before the one on the right, then yawned. "I might follow her example after you are settled."

"Please, do not forgo your rest on my account."

"Shall I have tea sent to your chamber? You might wish to rest a little before dinner, as well."

Catherine was content to let Eurydice set her schedule—and she did not mind the excuse to avoid Rhys. She had to decide how to proceed before encountering him again. "That also sounds like a most sensible notion. I thank you."

The door before them opened, revealing a housemaid on the point of departure. "It is all prepared as you specified, my lady," she said with a curtsey.

"Thank you, Sheldon," Eurydice said, then gestured for Catherine to precede her. The maid hastened down the hall with purpose. "I hope you will be at ease at Rockmorton Manor this Yuletide and perhaps even find inspiration of a kind."

Catherine might have asked for an explanation of that last comment, but she was awed by the bedchamber. It was generously proportioned and exquisitely furnished, with a commanding view over the garden and the stables beyond. Though the plants slumbered in this season, the small hedges on the borders of the paths were still green and it was evident that the design had a pleasing symmetry. The room itself was decorated in the palest pink with cream accents. It had polished furniture of dark wood, perhaps cherry, and a great fireplace with a stone mantle. Here, too, the greens had been brought in to provide a seasonal flourish on the mantle.

The bed was a large four-poster, piled with cushions and blankets, and Catherine guessed it would be a challenge to abandon it in the morning. A fire burned in the grate and there were a pair of comfortable chairs before the hearth. The large window had a padded seat where one could admire the view and heavy drapes to block the wind at night. To the right of the window was an elegant little writing desk; to the left was the door, perhaps to the room Rhys would occupy. The arrangements were both cozy and elegant.

"I cannot imagine being anything other than at ease in such a room," she said with a smile. "I thank you for your hospitality, Eurydice."

Eurydice beamed. "We have had so few guests. I wished to ensure you had a happy stay." The two women clasped hands and kissed each other's cheeks. "The library is downstairs, opposite the stairs, if you have need of another book. Gaines will show you the way."

"Thank you."

Eurydice left and Catherine removed her bonnet and cloak. Drawn to the window, she watched Rhys walk toward the stable with Montgomery—and yearned. She had never wanted to be anyone other than herself, but she would have given a great deal to be a woman desired by Rhys Bettencourt. The carriage had gone on before him and their host strolled with Rhys, gesturing as he talked about his estate. Both men were young, handsome and well-dressed, but it was Rhys that held Catherine's attention securely.

She remembered the night of their wedding as clearly as if it had just occurred.

CATHERINE COULD NOT SLEEP. She was abandoned in this luxurious house, where the servants whispered audibly that she did not deserve the master and where Foster was her only ally. She had asked to see the accounts when her husband fled their nuptials for his club and had been compelled to insist upon it. Numbers soothed her always and on this day, she needed a distraction. She reviewed the tallies and the entries again and again, certain of what she had found but unable to believe it.

The estate manager was embezzling funds from Trevelaine. They were small amounts, buried in myriad individual transactions, but the monthly tally was impressive. No one had noticed, not through all the months she reviewed that day. When she was informed that Mr. Jones, the estate manager, had served Rhys for the twenty years since he had gained his inheritance, and Rhys' father for at least ten before that, she feared the missing sum was substantial. She had checked and rechecked, tallied and reviewed, but she was right.

She doubted her husband would take the tidings well. She wondered whether he would believe her. It was possible he might not even care.

But Catherine cared. It was her fortune that was to repair his financial state, already she was convinced that Mr. Jones would quite merrily steal it as well.

She would stop the man herself, if need be.

But still, she did not sleep. Her grip tightened on the linens when she heard her husband in his adjacent chamber. The hour was late, so late that she hoped he would not come to her, but then the door to his rooms opened.

He did not bring a light. He did not speak to her. He smelled of brandy and smoke and she thought he staggered a bit when he approached the bed. She flinched when he lifted the covers and closed her eyes tightly, though he was only a looming shadow.

What was she supposed to do? She heard the bed creak as he settled upon it and felt the weight of his gaze upon her. She dared not look.

She could not make a sound and she knew she trembled.

"Hello, Catherine," he said in that glorious rumble that set her heart to pounding. There could be no doubt of his identity. "You might pretend to be glad I am here," he advised in a wicked whisper, then reached for her before she could consider what that might mean.

Catherine did not know how to respond but Rhys took command of the situation. His fingertips slid across her cheek, leaving a trail of fire in their wake, then pushed into her hair with a proprietary ease that thrilled her. He pulled her closer and kissed her, full on the lips, a salute so different from the polite buss they had shared at the wedding breakfast that Catherine could not believe the same word was used to describe both.

That kiss was like a taste of fire. She felt like tinder touched by the flame for the first time. His kiss awakened her, set her ablaze, and made her burn for more. His mouth slanted over hers, his kiss coaxing and caressing. It was a seductive kiss, so slow and deliberate, one that launched a pleasure beyond anything she had experienced before.

Catherine felt her mouth soften and she leaned closer to him instinctively, wanting only more of whatever he had to give. It was all new and slightly terrifying, but Rhys was so sure and she trusted his command. He leaned over her, all hardness and power, tucking her protectively beneath him, kissing her endlessly as the weight of his hand slid over her in a smooth caress. Catherine was lost in sensation, aware of a newfound desire when she felt the warmth of his hand beneath the hem of her chemise.

The slide of his palm over her bare skin was a revelation. The way he cupped her breast and ran his thumb over her nipple sent a surge through her that could not be denied. He rained kisses on her brow, her eyelids, the tip of her nose, then his mouth closed over hers again in demand. This kiss was harder and more urgent, demanding more. Catherine arched toward him, wanting to offer whatever he desired of her. She made a small sound of surrender and felt him chuckle in satisfaction, then his fingertips landed upon the most intimate part of her.

She gasped.

Rhys swallowed the sound with another alluring kiss, coaxing her to join him in this endeavor. Catherine forced the tension from her shoulders and chose again to follow his lead. His fingers moved then, caressing her and sending a wild abandon through her body. Catherine shivered to her toes and felt the hard strength of him beside her. She felt the heat grow within her as well as a troubling tumult and was aware of the dampness of her pleasure. She was uncertain, but Rhys was undaunted, so persuasive in his touch that she could not turn away.

The tension built steadily within her and she found her hands on his shoulders, her hair caught in his fist, his tongue diving into her mouth in a tantalizing dance that would drive her mad. Against every expectation, her hips bucked against his hand and when she might have regretted her boldness, his lips were against her ear, murmuring encouragement, branding her with his kiss.

She felt hardness against her hip but did not dare to explore. She was awash in sensation and powerless against its tide. She did not know how long the sweet torment lasted—it seemed both an eternity and a moment—but suddenly a ferocious wave swept through her, relentless and so potent that she cried out in ecstasy.

And then she was held close against him, the scent of his skin inundating her as she sought to slow the pounding of her heart. Something wet and warm had spilled against her hip at some point. Rhys held her close against his bare chest as she trembled in the aftermath, his arms strong around her, his breath in her hair.

He kissed her forehead when he relinquished his grip upon her long moments later.

And then he was gone, the door closing quietly behind him, Catherine alone in her own bed. She lay there for long moments, until the silence of the house wrapped around her, then rose to wash. Already, a part of her yearned to share that union again.

The curious thing about her husband's touch was that it was both satisfying and left her hungry for more. She could make no sense of it.

Would she conceive now? She supposed she must wait until her monthly courses were due to know for certain.

Either way, they were wed, for better and for worse, until death they did part.

CATHERINE SHOOK her head at the memory. Her courses had appeared on schedule and she had felt obliged to inform Rhys as much. He had not been surprised, which had confused her at the time. Since then any pretence of intimacy had been abandoned. It was clear the man found her repellent.

Until this day.

I have come to seduce you.

Even in recollection, Rhys' confession of this day made Catherine's heart leap. How wondrous it must be for a woman to know she was desired for her own self, but that would never be her fate. It had to be her fortune that drove his choice.

The question was what she intended to do about it.

She did not truly wish to leave Rhys—even the occasional glimpse of him was irresistible—but neither did she wish to continue as they had. She hadn't expected love, but she had expected children, and without them, she might as well have been another estate manager or housekeeper.

Falling in love with her husband had left her greedy for more.

Foster appeared then and briskly began to unpack. The maid was full of admiration of the kitchens and the house, chattering happily about the surprise of the baron's presence as she set all to rights. When she was done, Catherine dismissed her with the instruction to return at seven to help her dress for dinner.

The books Eurydice had promised were in a neat pile on the window seat. Catherine lifted the first one. She nodded without surprise, because she had also enjoyed it. She set it aside and considered the next, a work unfamiliar to her. She retrieved her glasses to glance at the first page and thought she would like it. She might have moved to one of the chairs before the fire to read more, but noticed a leaf of paper atop the third book. It had been hidden between the volumes.

It had to be a note from Eurydice.

An excerpt from The Ladies' Essential Guide to the Art of Seduction.

It cannot be denied that in matters of intimacy between husband and wife, a gently-bred lady has no recourse to information, save her spouse's counsel. Many men decline to provide any tutelage, leaving their wives dissatisfied though those ladies cannot clearly identify the cause. Such is the result of a lack of education in matters of intimacy. This volume intends to fill the deficit by ensuring that ladies of merit know what to expect in the marital bed, as well as how to induce their husbands to join them there frequently and with enthusiasm.

Catherine turned the sheet of paper over. It was just one page, not a volume, and she knew all of the current books of conduct available for young women. This most certainly was not from any of them. By and large, they were composed by men, and their primary concern was the defense of virtue. Catherine thought them dull.

This was definitely different.

She did not recognize the neat handwriting, though it was feminine in its elegant slant and frequent flourishes. She did not think it was Eurydice's hand, though they had exchanged only a few notes. Eurydice had a simpler style.

Was someone in the household composing a book? Perhaps Eurydice herself was writing a volume of advice for married ladies. What a remarkable notion! Catherine had a moment's doubt as to whether she should continue to read, but she suspected the page had been specifically left for her.

The unknown author doubtless wanted Catherine's opinion of the work.

A housemaid knocked and Catherine hid the page inside a book before the girl entered. Her tea was delivered, along with some fresh scones. The maid ensured that Catherine had all she desired, then departed. A light rain began to patter against the window again. Catherine retreated to that inviting chair by the fire, took off her boots and put her feet up on a stool. She sipped her tea and continued to read.

Upon tempting the gentlemanly gaze...

Men are greatly enticed by appearances, and a lady of good sense can use this trait in her favor when courting the attention of the gentleman of her choice. The lady intent on claiming a gentleman's eye would be advised to take note of what pleases him so she may provide an alluring vision. This is best done with subtlety.

For example, if a gentleman has commented in the past upon a lady's choice of dress or the style of her hair, she might choose this dress or style her hair thus when she particularly desires his attention. He may conclude that she is seeking his favor and respond accordingly—or he may simply be drawn to her side by his attraction, without recalling the previous instance. Similarly, if a gentleman has surrendered a gift to the lady in question, he will be pleased when she wears it. Indeed, he may interpret such a choice as an invitation for more of his attention.

Catherine put down the page and stared into the fire, her heart fluttering. Was this the advice she needed? Was it possible that Rhys had not come to her because he thought her disinterested in his attentions?

What if she encouraged him? It would be uncommonly bold, but would ensure there was no doubt of her expectations. If the possibility of removing the impasse between them was in her hands, Catherine felt obliged to try. Indeed, the prospect of being so daring made her heart skip.

She began to read avidly again, wishing there was more than one page.

Be aware that many gentlemen are circumspect in revealing their more earthly desires. Watch his eyes for a flicker of interest or a change of hue: some men's eyes grow darker when they are aroused. A gentleman's gaze will return repeatedly to a lady of interest, or may even remain locked upon her despite all other attractions in his vicinity. His lips may tighten. His eyes may seem to glitter and there will be an intensity about him that was absent previously. If his nostrils flare, his interest is well and truly snared. An attentive gentleman is an interested gentleman...

~

CATHERINE WAS LATE FOR DINNER. Rhys could not fathom it. His wife was the most punctual woman he had ever known. He admired that she never kept anyone waiting and thought it a most courteous trait. He had heard her chatting to Foster in her adjacent room while he had changed his linen. What could be the cause of her delay? The delay seemed doubly long since he was so intent upon speaking with her again. On this night, he would charm her, one way or the other.

Rhys sipped his sherry with impatience, admired Montgomery's new favored hound yet again, and tried to avoid his rising sense of guilt. The sherry dulled it admirably, just as brandy had done on his wedding night.

There was a shuffling on the stairs, interrupted by the regular thump of a cane, then a crooked figure appeared in the doorway of the drawing room. The arrival had a maid with her, one who supported the elbow of her charge. This had to be Montgomery's aunt, Mrs. Delilah Oliver, whom Rhys had not yet met.

She was a spectacularly hideous woman. She resembled nothing more than a toad. Her hair was copious and grey, obviously a wig and one arranged with great care in the ringlets and style of bygone years. It looked the worse for wear and Rhys wondered what manner of vermin resided within it. Her dress was of elaborately embroidered olive green silk, a color that did not favor her in the least. Indeed, it made her complexion appear to be even more of a yellow hue than it was. The dress was in a style he recalled his grandmother wearing, with a full skirt and tightly fitted sleeves and bodice, a choice that did not disguise this lady's stoutness a whit.

But it was her face that made Rhys yearn to look away. It was so wrinkled and of such a ghastly hue that he could readily believe that one of the witches from Shakespeare's Scottish play had come to life in Montgomery's home. Her nose was long and hooked, her brow low, her cheeks sagged and yet, there was a black beauty mark stuck to her cheek. Had she once been pretty? Rhys could not imagine so. Her lips were painted a vivid pink, as if that would make her look young. It was a false hope for there were no less than a dozen coarse white hairs sprouting from her chin, and a trio of warts beside her nose.

Her one remarkable feature was her eyes, which were a clear green. They reminded Rhys of something or someone, but he could not think of who or what.

She wore gloves of a mustard hue and he was glad not to be able to see her gnarled hands. The misshapen dimension of them beneath the gloves was sufficient to have him avert his gaze. A veritable treasury of sparkling gems rested upon her ample bosom, but even Rhys could see that they were paste.

The crone was guided to the best chair before the fire and sat down abruptly, as if her knees had given out beneath her considerable weight. She exhaled lustily and peered at the men with what might have been hostility. The maid retreated.

"Aunt Delilah," Montgomery said politely, bowing to her. "How marvelous you look this evening."

Marvelous? Rhys blinked, certain they could not be looking at the same woman.

Montgomery gestured. "I must present my friend,

Mr. Rhys Bettencourt, Baron Trevelaine. Bettencourt, this is Mrs. Delilah Oliver. Recently widowed, she has returned from the Continent and deigned to spend the holidays with us." He smiled at his guest. "She is my grandmother's cousin, a long-lost relation newly found again."

"The pleasure is mine, Mrs. Oliver." Rhys bowed.

The old lady surveyed him, squinting as she did as much. "So, you're the rakehell tamed by a bluestocking bride," she said to Rhys' surprise. "I heard the tale of your reformation and to be sure, sir, I expected you to be older and less finely featured."

Rhys did not know how to reply to such a comment and found himself speechless for the first time in his life.

"Would you care for a sherry, Aunt?" Montgomery asked.

"A proper one, if you please, not a thimble like you gave me last night," the lady in question said, her tone rising querulously. "I know that the markets are not what they were, but I grow no younger. I will savor my pleasures while I can and *you* can afford to indulge me."

Rhys would have wagered that this cousin had sought out Montgomery for the sake of her personal comfort at Yuletide. It was not his place to comment, so he bit his tongue.

Montgomery agreed smoothly, apparently untroubled by his guest's manners. "A large sherry for Aunt Delilah, if you please, Gaines."

"Immediately, sir."

The sherry was served to the old lady who clutched it in one twisted claw as if she feared it might be claimed by another. Eurydice appeared in the doorway then, looking rosy and happy. She greeted Rhys and Mrs. Oliver, then beckoned to Montgomery. He went to his wife's side, likely to confer about some domestic matter, leaving Rhys with the old woman who was slurping her sherry and smacking her lips after each sip. Indeed, she made it vanish more quickly than the worst sot in a gaming hell. He was quite certain a hound would have consumed it more quietly.

Rhys could not abandon her, though, as there were no other guests in the drawing room. Where was Catherine?

Mrs. Oliver peered at Rhys again. "Have you abandoned your wife, sir?"

"It appears she has been delayed."

"And not by you, it is clear," the old lady said with a snort of disapproval. "I would have expected more from a man of your reputation. My third husband insisted upon trying the bed each time we arrived in a new location." She sighed with rapture and Rhys could not imagine her nude, much less engaged in intimate relations. He did not even want to imagine it. "I could never wait to undertake a journey with him. We were always late for dinner. Both of us! Ha!" She drained her glass, holding it out to Gaines in silent demand. The glass was immediately refilled. Mrs. Oliver eyed Rhys anew. "How many children do you have?"

"None, Mrs. Oliver."

"None? *None.*" She shook her head with disgust. "You are recently married, then?"

Rhys cleared his throat, uncertain why this woman thought she had the right to so interrogate him. "We have been wed these two years."

"*Two* years? Two?! Did I hear you correctly?" When Rhys nodded, she shook her head with disgust. "Then what delays you? Even a baron needs a son, if not two or three." She wagged her finger at him. "Time runs swiftly, though you are too young to believe as much. Why delay a moment longer? You should miss dinner this very night to entertain your wife!"

"That would scarcely be appropriate," Rhys began but she had already gestured to Montgomery.

"*He* fulfilled his duties quickly," she said with approval. "But the men in our family always understood their obligations. Ha!" She drank noisily from her glass, considering Rhys with disfavor. She could not have been more vulgar if she tried. It was difficult to believe that Montgomery had any connection with such a woman.

"Has the cat seized your tongue?" she demanded when she had drained her glass's contents. "Time was a gentleman knew how to make conversation and entertain a lady. You appear to be as ornamental as the Christmas greens." She cackled to herself again, setting down the glass on the table unsteadily. "Perhaps it is no mystery why your wife evades the tedium of your company."

As ornamental as the Christmas greens?

Tedium?

Rhys bristled. "How many children do you have, Mrs. Oliver?" The question was rude, to his thinking, but turnabout was fair play.

"Seven!" she declared with gusto. "All married, with three couples expecting soon enough. Ten grandchildren." Her tone was triumphant, then her eyes narrowed slightly. "You see why I think you are slow to enter the game. Are you ill? Is there something amiss?" She gestured toward his trousers with her cane.

Rhys took a step back, half-thinking she might poke him, and she made a curious choking sound.

Was she laughing at him?

"Madame, I believe your query is unseemly…"

She leaned closer, eyes gleaming. "The wife then, is it?" she asked in a hoarse whisper. "Barren? Cold as ice?" She nodded wisely. "You should get another. A mistress, even. A legacy can be settled on a bastard if he is the sole one."

Rhys inhaled sharply but she had seized her glass again. Indeed, she was loudly sucking at the last few drops like a woman dying of thirst.

"Are you being impertinent, Aunt?" Montgomery asked easily as he rejoined them. He smiled as he glanced at Rhys. "No doubt time will ensure the conception of an heir for Trevelaine."

"Time? It is not *time* that brings babies, sir, nor is it the wind or even Providence." Mrs. Oliver spoke with conviction. "There is only one deed that will do it. I would expect that your education had been sufficiently thorough for you to know that."

Rhys did not know what to say so he sipped his sherry. The clock in the hall chimed eight, but there was no sign of Catherine.

Was something amiss?

"I wonder whether my wife has fallen asleep," Rhys said to Eurydice, who also glanced toward the stairs. It would not be all bad to have an excuse to leave this harridan's side. "She might have just intended to close her eyes for a moment."

"Or she might have lost herself in a good book," Montgomery said.

Eurydice smiled at him. "I know how readily either can happen."

In that moment, there was a flurry of footsteps on the stairs.

It could not be Catherine, Rhys thought even as he turned to look. She always walked with measured steps, the very essence of decorum.

"The time!" the arrival said, her words breathless.

But Rhys could only stare.

CHAPTER 3

It was Catherine but not Catherine. Something was sufficiently changed to make her look like another woman. She might have been a flirtatious and pretty sister, but Catherine's sisters were neither. This was Catherine, to be sure.

She was wearing a dress of pale gold silk with embroidery upon the hem, and Rhys realized with a start that it was the same one she had worn for their wedding. Like Catherine herself, it was subtle and he was struck by how perfectly it suited her.

All the same, there was something different. Rhys did not recall the garment appearing so provocative. The bodice dipped lower than he recalled, leaving the top of her breasts exposed. Catherine always wore a lace fichu over her modest dresses. On this night, the perfection of her figure was revealed to all. Seeing so much of Catherine's skin was highly distracting, to be sure.

It was both beguiling and enticing.

Her hair was also different, the curls arranged more softly so they tumbled down her neck and shoulders. There was a disarray about her that was uncharacteristic, a flush in her cheeks and a sparkle of excitement in her eyes. The combination suited her so well that Rhys could not imagine why anyone would ever think her plain—or like a statue. She had abandoned her glasses and he could see the glorious blue of her eyes more clearly. She wore the garnet red shawl that he had bought for her the previous Christmas, a hue that suited her to perfection. Indeed, the candlelight favored her admirably, making her look like a goddess who had stepped down to earth.

The greatest difference, though, was Catherine's smile. She looked happy, triumphant even, as she watched him stare. Rhys was dazzled and did not hide his reaction a whit. Catherine's gaze clung to his for a heart-stopping moment, her smile increasing the smallest increment and making his own heart gallop.

He bent low over her hand. "My lady," he murmured and felt her gloved hand tremble in his grasp.

To his dismay, she did not speak to him.

"I do apologize," she said to Eurydice and Montgomery with the smile that Rhys believed could melt the coldest of hearts. "I did not mean to keep you all waiting."

"Did you fall asleep?" Rhys asked, wanting her attention again. He bent to retrieve the end of her shawl, lifting it to her shoulder. When he tucked it over her elbow, he was struck by her beauty. Her lips were a perfect ruddy bow and the dark sweep of her lashes—so unexpected with her fair coloring—was utterly lovely.

What fool had warned him that Catherine Carruthers was plain?

She smiled up at him, eyes aglow, and his heart thundered. How could her lips appear so soft? And what was the alluring scent that rose from her skin, inviting him to move closer? He wished with all his heart that they might have been alone in this moment, that he could have swept her off her feet and headed for her chamber.

Or at least kissed more than her hand.

"You are right, sir. I did," she confessed, her voice low and soft. She looked up at him through her lashes, then, wonder of wonders, laid her hand on his arm. "You always anticipate me so perfectly, Rhys." The sound of his name upon her lips was a delight unexpected. She leaned closer, holding his gaze, granting him a view of her cleavage. With her expression so alight and her perfume enveloping him in a cloud, Rhys was enchanted.

It would be so easy to bend down and touch his mouth to hers, to pull her closer and feel her softness against him, to taste her sweetly. But this was Catherine. She was neither affectionate nor emotional, and thus not susceptible to whatever charm he possessed. She also would not welcome any breach of propriety in the presence of others.

"Thank you so much for this stole. It was a thoughtful gift."

"I knew the color would favor you well."

"But I never wear red."

"All the same, it is a good hue for you, Catherine," he said, for he believed it.

"You sound like the dressmaker I visited with Prudence," she teased and he laughed.

"Shall I change my occupation?"

She flushed. "I think not, sir."

"Then perhaps I will simply counsel you."

"Oh." Time stood still as Rhys watched Catherine smile just for him. Then incredibly, he felt her fingertips slide along his arm. The caress sent a jolt through him, one that made him yearn to possess her completely. "I would like that," she whispered.

"Then you would have to endure my companionship at the dressmaker," he teased, smiling when the suggestion obviously flustered her. It pleased her as well, for her eyes sparkled.

"I shall endeavor to endure it, s—Rhys," she said so softly that only he could hear her words, then cast a mischievous glance through her lashes. Her grip tightened upon his hand and he knew she would turn away to their host and hostess.

"I do apologize," she said in her normal tones to Montgomery. "I have not met your aunt."

She moved away and Rhys felt bereft. He blinked and watched her float toward the dining room, appreciating for the first time how his life would change if Catherine left.

In that moment, Rhys knew with startling clarity that he did not want Catherine to leave his house or his side. He wanted a marriage in every way, yet he knew that if he argued his own cause now, she would believe he wished only to secure her dowry and fortune.

And then there was the curse.

He had to convince her to stay, but the only way to do that was to put her very life in peril.

The very prospect turned Rhys' blood cold. It was a wretchedly inconvenient moment to realize that he loved his wife with all his heart.

What was he to do?

COULD TRIUMPH BE WON SO EASILY?

Esmeralda was disappointed by the prospect. She had been looking forward to a game of cat-and-mouse for the entire fortnight of the visit. If Bettencourt went to his wife's bed on the first night, the entertainment would be vastly curtailed—though she would not quibble with success.

On the one hand, Esmeralda was enormously reassured by the baron's susceptibility to his wife's charms that night at dinner. He was clearly enamored of the baroness, perhaps even as much as the lady in question was in love with him. If there was an impediment to their union, it was not a lack of affection.

That was a formidable relief.

Eurydice, on Esmeralda's advice, had seated Bettencourt between herself and Mrs. Oliver. Since they were five, there was an empty space, which was between Eurydice and Lady Catherine. This left Bettencourt at the opposite corner of the table from his wife and it was not a small table, being customarily set for twelve. It was delicious to note the baron's torment and to prod him at intervals.

The man deserved no less to Esmeralda's view for so denying his wife these two years.

Even better, the baroness had taken Esmeralda's written advice with unexpected enthusiasm. Esmeralda guessed the choice of her dress had been a deliberate one, for Bettencourt had been clearly startled by the sight of the garment. The details were unimportant. It was sufficiently satisfactory to watch the lady, who had been so subdued on her arrival, sparkle as Montgomery flirted shamelessly with her.

That too had been on Esmeralda's suggestion.

Truly, she had expected Bettencourt to be a harder prey to land, but she supposed all was well that ended well. When the ladies rose and went to the library, Lady Trevelaine came around the table to help dear Mrs. Oliver as her husband watched her avidly.

The lady blew her husband a playful kiss from the doorway.

Perfect. She was an ideal pupil. Esmeralda was already concocting the next note the baroness would discover in her room.

"I wonder, Catherine, if you might be interested in a small excursion on the morrow," Eurydice said once the three women were comfortably seated by the drawing room fire and tea had been poured.

Esmeralda decided it was time for her to be inattentive. She coughed and fussed over her blanket, then made every show of falling asleep. She snorted then began to snore loudly.

She was well aware of the indulgent smile exchanged by the other women.

"An excursion?" Lady Catherine asked.

"The village, Rockmorton Fell, is but two miles away and there is a delightful apothecary shop there. The proprietor's wife is rumored to be a witch, which is all nonsense, of course, but she makes charms. I have a fancy for one to bring good luck in the birth."

"Surely you, of all women, are not superstitious?" There was indulgence in the baroness' tone.

"Surely not," Eurydice agreed easily. "But still, a little extra luck could not hurt."

There was a pause before the guest asked her question. "Are you afraid?"

"No. I have read every book I could find on the subject—there is now quite a collection in the library—and my sister has given me a great deal of advice. I am certain all will go well." Eurydice spoke as if she could make it so, simply by her declaration, and Esmeralda hoped all did proceed well.

"But a charm would be welcome all the same," her guest suggested warmly.

"I thought you might like to see the village, as well. It is lovely, but small. There are two elderly ladies who have been unwell, I understand, and I will take them some of Mrs. Purcell's soup."

"And the gentlemen?"

"Montgomery is determined to hunt on the morrow, as it is supposed to be fair."

"I should be pleased to accompany you," the baroness said.

The carriage would be arranged, just as Esmeralda had devised. She had a great fondness for carriages as locations for liaisons herself. The women discussed the arrangements, though Esmeralda knew full well that Eurydice would not go at the last moment. They had planned as much.

All they had to contrive yet was Bettencourt's presence in the carriage. Even if he succumbed on the first night, victory had to be secured.

SEBASTIAN WATCHED his friend consume yet another glass of fine brandy. The ladies had retired to the library after dinner, leaving the two gentlemen in the dining room as the candles burned down. Bettencourt seemed determined to empty the entire bottle of brandy before his host's eyes.

He could not recall when he had ever seen Bettencourt so troubled.

He certainly had never seen Bettencourt stare so intently at his wife over a dinner table before. The lady had been more vivacious than Sebastian had ever known her to be, a surprise since she had been quiet on their previous encounters. He had underestimated her, it was clear, always having thought she was a quiet and practical woman. On this night, though, she had smiled and jested, she had flirted and she had laughed—and her husband had been unable to look away.

Even Mrs. Oliver's noisy consumption of every morsel had not broken the spell.

It seemed that Eurydice's scheme was finding early success.

"I would not deny you all the brandy you desire, but on this night, you cannot wish to sleep," Sebastian noted finally.

Bettencourt gave him a look. Sebastian's old friend was the most handsome of all of his companions from school, but also could be inscrutable. There was a shadow in his eyes this night and a grimness in his manner that was unfamiliar, one that was at odds with the merry mood of his wife.

"Whyever not?" Bettencourt demanded.

"I do not wish to be outspoken, but it appears your wife wishes to entice you to her bed."

"I must decline," his companion said and filled his glass.

Sebastian felt his eyes narrow. He knew that if he asked, Bettencourt might change the subject, for his friend was inclined to keep his secrets. When first he had heard Eurydice's tale, Sebastian had been certain there must be some cause of nature behind it all, one that could not be helped by man or woman. But after seeing Bettencourt this night, he had a feeling he knew the reason for their barren marriage.

"You cannot believe that foolish curse," he said quietly.

"Why should I not?" his friend demanded with a glare.

"Because it is mere superstition. You said as much yourself."

"That was twenty years ago. I have learned my own error."

"Your father made you promise to wed a woman you did not hold in affection. He wanted you to ensure the succession thus, since the beloved wives of the Bettencourt family invariably die in delivery of an heir."

Sebastian shook his head. "Nonsense! You know that kind of rumor is never well-founded."

"My mother died in the birthing of me, and my father never recovered from her loss," Bettencourt insisted. "He wished to spare me the anguish he experienced."

"All well-intentioned, but I recall how you laughed about his demand when you returned to school." They had been all of twelve years of age, living at school, when Bettencourt had been summoned to his father's deathbed. Bettencourt was the first of them to be possessed of his legacy and title. Oh, they had been envious! "You have an alluring wife and she appears to be willing. Why do you not yet have an heir?"

Bettencourt sighed. "I accepted the marriage with Catherine, believing that I could never love a woman whose fortune had been earned in trade. It was a practical match—"

"One that the Duke of Haynesdale gave you no choice to decline."

Bettencourt nodded. "I was proud and unkind, but Catherine has taught me the error of my thinking. The day of our marriage, she took it upon herself to review the accounting of my holdings while I was at Brook's..."

"You went to your club on your wedding day?"

"The match was arranged," Bettencourt said grimly. "There was no affection between us and I thought it unlikely there would be any." He turned his glass in his hand and Sebastian wondered he admitted all of the truth. "The next day, Catherine presented me with a tallying of the sum my estate manager had appropriated from my funds in recent years. I was outraged that she would accuse a trusted man so long in our family service. I insisted she was wrong. She insisted there would be more when previous years were checked and we argued. She challenged me then to take the matter to our solicitor. You should have seen her. She was furious with me." He frowned in recollection.

"You were insulted by her accusations."

"I was enthralled by her. She had shown no emotion at our wedding or the breakfast afterward, and might have been wrought of stone. The next day, she was alight with her fury, like she had a twin sister." Bettencourt shook his head. "It was unexpected and *most* attractive."

Montgomery guessed the truth then, but was uncertain Bettencourt had realized his affection for his own wife.

They sat in silence for a long moment, the crackle of the fire the sole sound between them. Montgomery cleared his throat. "I will guess that she was right about the estate manager."

Bettencourt nodded. "They summoned Mr. Jones to an interview and he confessed it all. By the end of the week, there was a plan to repay the stolen funds and my solicitors were highly impressed with my wife's skill."

"Why did she even delve into the books?"

"She asked to see them, since her dowry was intended to save my estates. I believe she feared the fortune bestowed upon her by her father might be insufficient." Bettencourt shook his head. "It would have been if she had not uncovered the truth. Jones would have simply stolen it, too."

"How could you not have known?"

"Recall that I was twelve when I came into my inheritance and I had never been taught to manage money myself. It gave joy to my sisters when I indulged them. When there was less than expected, I thought I had been too frivolous. It never occurred to me that my father's estate agent had betrayed his trust and then mine." Bettencourt stared into the fire. "I never knew such contentment as when Catherine and I spent each day in the library, reviewing the books and setting budgets. It was highly satisfactory labor, and Catherine was remarkable." His voice dropped low. "Now we meet monthly. You will laugh that I look forward to the exchange."

"It only makes sense to admire her gift and intellect. You build a future together."

"Do we?" Bettencourt reached for the bottle again.

Something about his friend's manner fed Sebastian's suspicions. He leaned closer, knowing it was forward for him to ask the question but hoping that they might share one more confidence. "Have you *ever* visited your wife's bed?" he asked softly.

Bettencourt looked at him, his expression hard. "Once, but not in the way you mean." He looked up. "It was insufficient, but I had been at Brook's..." He waved a hand. "She plans to return to her father's home in the new year. It seems she prefers his books to me. I came here to change her thinking, but now, now I wonder whether she deserves better than what I can give her."

Sebastian pushed to his feet, impatient with the discussion. "Nonsense! Did you not see how your wife looked at mine? She wishes for a child, Bettencourt, if only to do her duty to you. How can you deny her that?"

"How can you imperil your wife's life for your pleasure and your property?" Bettencourt demanded sharply.

"She is not greatly at risk."

His friend shook his head. "Wait until she delivers of the child. You will change your mind when her screams fill these halls."

Sebastian sat down opposite his guest. "The endeavor is not without risk, to be sure, but Eurydice is healthy and young. Her sister has delivered safely of so many children that I have lost track of them all."

"I make no jest," Bettencourt growled.

"Nor do I," Sebastian said, sobering. "I have hired two midwives and the finest doctor in Cornwall arrives after the Yule as a houseguest. I have ensured that all recommendations have been followed and will do my utmost to ensure my wife's welfare."

Bettencourt slanted a glance his way. "But you cannot guarantee it."

Sebastian chose his words with care. "Women deliver children safely all the time, Bettencourt."

"But some die," his friend insisted.

"Nothing says that Eurydice will be one of them."

"Nothing says she will not be."

"You should talk to the baroness," Sebastian advised. "Find the solution with her aid."

But Bettencourt shook his head. "Be glad, Montgomery, that your family does not share the curse of mine. Without that pledge to my father and the curse, my path this night would be clear." Before Sebastian could think of what to say, Bettencourt had left the dining room. "Forbes!" he roared in the foyer, then began to climb the stairs.

Sebastian stared after him, amazed. Their lack of a child was not because Bettencourt disdained his wife. It was because he had fallen in love with her, against his every expectation, and despite his pledge to his father. And if she conceived, Bettencourt feared the family curse would ensure her demise.

Worse, their marriage was not consummated. The lady likely believed that whatever had happened on the wedding night had been sufficient. He saw now the justification for Eurydice's outrage that women were told so little about intimacy.

But if Catherine did not know that the match was

unconsummated, she did not realize that it could be annulled. Sebastian doubted that Bettencourt wanted his wife to know she could take complete leave of the marriage and him, given his love for her.

All the same, it was only right that her happiness be considered as well. And Bettencourt could not be said to be content himself.

Sebastian felt a conflict over his choices, but he knew the Duke of Haynesdale would not take kindly to this revelation. That man had arranged Bettencourt's match and was fond of the bride.

The truth had to be shared.

If Bettencourt could not resolve his situation, Sebastian knew the duke would do it for him.

In that moment, Eurydice and Catherine came to the door of the drawing room, their faces alight with curiosity. Sebastian could hear the loud echo of Mrs. Oliver's contented snoring. He was struck to silence by the sadness that claimed Catherine's expression as she watched her husband vanish into the shadows of the corridor above. Her shoulders drooped and the lively companion he had admired earlier was banished. She turned back to the drawing room, leaving Eurydice in the doorway alone and Sebastian knew that Bettencourt's was not the only heart that had been claimed.

"Whatever is amiss?" Eurydice asked in a whisper. "Why does he retire?"

"The brandy was stronger than he anticipated," Sebastian said, not wanting to burden her with Bettencourt's fears so close to her own time. He smiled and took her arm, tugging her close. "He will regret it more in the morning. Is that horrific sound from Mrs. Oliver?"

Eurydice laughed and leaned against him. "She is having far too much enjoyment out of this," she confided in a whisper.

"I suspect she is not alone in that," he murmured, drawing his wife close as Eurydice laughed aloud. He would do whatever was necessary to ensure her safety, even surrender his own life instead.

And in the meantime, he would write to the duke.

CATHERINE PREPARED FOR BED, her hopes dashed by Rhys' state. It was their wedding day all over again. Why would he claim to be intent on seducing her, then forget his own vow? Was she so abhorrent to him that he had to seek consolation from brandy?

She did not even attend to Foster's chatter about the gossip below-stairs. Where had she gone wrong? The counsel from *The Ladies' Essential Guide to the Art of Seduction* had been flawless. Catherine had abandoned the lace fichu she always wore and had Foster dress her hair differently. By good fortune, she had brought the very dress she had worn for her wedding day.

She had never expected that Rhys would respond with such alacrity. She had been halfway certain he wouldn't even notice, but he hadn't been able to look away from her. It had been thrilling to have his undivided attention and the change made her realize that she was not without power in their relationship. His attention had filled her with newfound confidence and a hope for the night ahead.

But he was drunk and she was alone.

Again.

Foster departed and Catherine went to the small pile of books on the window seat. She had left the page where she had discovered it and wondered if it might offer more advice that she had missed.

But the page was missing. Catherine fanned through the books, checked the writing table and the drawers, searched the entire room, but that page had vanished as if it had never been.

How curious.

She felt bereft, as if she had lost an ally only recently gained, though that was whimsical. She took one of Eurydice's recommended books and settled before the fire to read.

She would not sleep soon, to be sure.

~

CATHERINE HEARD the missive slide under the door.

It was very early, the sky only beginning to brighten, and the house was quiet. No one had come to light the fire as yet, but she was comfortably warm in the great bed. She had not slept well, her thoughts spinning all the night long.

What should she do?

When she heard the minute sound, Catherine looked toward the door. There was a folded sheet of paper on the rug just inside the door. She rose from bed and went to pick it up, thinking it was from Eurydice. Perhaps their excursion would be delayed for another day. She unfolded the paper and read the first line.

An excerpt from The Ladies' Essential Guide to the Art of Seduction.

It was a different note than the one that had vanished.

There was *more*.

She could not hear a sound in the corridor, though she opened the door and looked. There was no sign of anyone, though she could hear a maid emerging from the servants' stairs with her bucket and coal.

Catherine closed the door and leaned against it,

heart leaping as she unfolded the paper again and began to read.

Upon the merit of audacity and surprise...

Many gentlemen are creatures of routine, following a schedule of entertainments and obligations. Many others, particularly those born to affluence, become accustomed to influencing circumstances around them, or even actively changing the course of events. These tendencies often manifest vigorously in matters of intimacy: gentlemen always know what they like and as a rule, initiate endeavors that result in their satisfaction. That said, however, the vast majority of gentleman respond remarkably well to a surprise of amorous nature.

For example, ladies are taught to await their husband's initiation of relations. We also learn that we are expected to endure these intervals, but are seldom advised to enjoy them, much less invite them. It is this writer's experience that all gentleman delight in advances from a lady held in their affection, particularly when such actions are unexpected.

Boldness is often well-rewarded.

A word also upon the merit of interruption. There is nothing like an incomplete act to leave a gentleman desirous of more. Consider the possibility of enticing him to a point and no further, thereby ensuring his attendance upon you, the better to finish what has been begun.

Catherine read the page twice then folded it as she considered its counsel. Even reading the counsel increased her confidence of success. Could she be so audacious as to invite Rhys' attention with a touch? She had caressed his arm the night before and his eyes had darkened. Indeed, his whole being had tensed with the avidity of his attention—and he had not been able to tear his gaze from her during dinner. The advice had been right about that.

The sum of their intimate moments was almost nil and her experience of amorous pleasures limited, but Catherine recalled that kiss on their wedding night. It had been lovely and languorous.

Sadly, she had not been kissed by Rhys since.

What if she kissed him? The prospect made her heart skip. For two years, he had—at most—touched his lips to her gloved hand. It was a more formal gesture but still such rare contact made her blood simmer.

Catherine read the advice again. Another kiss. It was a small thing to venture. If nothing else, she would know then whether the first had been such a marvel or whether she had embellished the memory.

She heard sounds from the adjacent room, including the splash of water followed by the rumble of her husband's voice.

She would do it while Rhys was in his bath, the better to ensure that he could not evade her words. He would be trapped. Her pulse fluttered. Having him at her mercy seemed both dangerous and delightful.

Catherine swallowed and reached for her robe, then froze to stare.

Her practical woolen dressing robe, which she had left at the foot of the bed, had been replaced with a shimmering confection of azure silk. The garment was soft and light, and it shone as she lifted it in her hands. It felt like heaven against her bare skin, which surely was the intention of the donor. It was so light and clung to her curves like a second skin, and the sensation of it made her feel like a seductive goddess.

Who had left it for her? Catherine neither knew nor cared. She brushed out her hair and abandoned her slippers. She lifted her chin and stared at the connecting door, gathering her resolve.

She would kiss Rhys now.

CHAPTER 4

$\mathcal{R}$hys' bedchamber had a fine bed and a fire that heated the room to perfection. Had he been lacking a thunderous headache, he might have enjoyed its comforts, but on this day, he wanted only to close his eyes against the light and slumber until noon.

Sadly, he was not to be so fortunate.

He had received a note with his tea that his host expected him to hunt at nine, so he rose with reluctance as Forbes filled a tub with hot water. It was set before the hearth and he sank into the welcome warmth.

What was he to do about Catherine?

Just then, there was a brisk rap upon the door to the adjoining chamber. Forbes did not manage to completely hide his surprise, but no one waited for the valet to answer the summons. Catherine herself swept immediately into the room, as if she did so as a matter of routine.

Rhys had never seen her in his bedroom, in any house, and he had never seen her enter any room with such a flourish. There had to be something amiss. He began to stand before he realized he was nude and she had never seen him thus. He sat down again promptly, sending the water surging over the lip of the tub. Forbes was staring between the two of them.

Catherine, to his astonishment, wore a dressing robe he had never seen before. The blue silk clung to her figure so lovingly that she must have been nude beneath it, a most intriguing and distracting circumstance. Her hair was loose, hanging in a blonde tangle of curls to her waist that invited his caress, and her cheeks were flushed. She looked magnificent. Rhys felt his headache fade and his interest rise.

Belatedly, he noticed that Catherine's expression was particularly resolute.

"Would you spare a moment of your time, sir?" she asked tightly, addressing the far corner of the ceiling.

"Of course." Rhys found himself fascinated and intrigued.

"You will leave us for a moment, Forbes," she said, her gaze flicking to the valet. Her tone left no possibility of the man doing otherwise.

Forbes was visibly astonished, but he complied.

As soon as the valet was gone, Catherine's gaze locked upon Rhys so fixedly that his mouth went dry. She could have been a battle maiden, girded for war, and he wondered how she might ensure his demise. He rather thought he might enjoy whatever torment she might inflict upon him. "I trust you are recovered from your indulgence of last evening, sir?" Her tone was oddly formal in the circumstance.

Rhys smiled, trying to charm her. "I have rather a headache, but I came by it honestly."

His effort failed.

"Indeed." She licked her lips, glanced at that ceiling corner again, and flushed more deeply. Rhys did not even dare to blink, lest he miss a detail.

He also, remarkably, did not know what to do.

To his shock, Catherine clenched her fists and

crossed the room to him with decisive steps. He might have commented upon that she seemed to be compelled toward him against her will, but she bent down. Her robe gaped open to offer a view of her splendid breasts and he forgot whatever he might have said. She was unaware of her own copious charms, which made Rhys' heart clench and his desire roar. Her fair hair tumbled over one shoulder, the ends landing in the bath water, but she did not draw back. She was so close and almost nude and everything within Rhys demanded that he act upon that opportunity.

As he stared into her eyes, Rhys recognized that all he desired was before him, yet to partake of it would cost him Catherine herself.

That wretched curse! He gripped the sides of the tub and strove to dismiss his every base urge.

He failed.

He failed yet further when she untied the robe and let it fall to the floor in a flutter of blue silk. For the first time ever, he looked upon her nude, and it was a glorious sight. His gaze roved over her, his chest was tight, and Rhys had no words.

"Your eyes are darker," Catherine murmured, then smiled just a little. "And your jaw is tense. Indeed, I think your eyes glitter a little." Her words made no sense to Rhys but her tone was triumphant. Against every expectation, she touched her fingertips to his chin and ran them along the line of his jaw toward his mouth, tentative and yet wildly seductive. Her eyes were impossibly blue and her lips were invitingly rosy and soft.

Who was this glorious temptress?

He was hers for the taking, whatever her identity.

"Are you agitated, sir?"

"Very," Rhys ceded tightly before he could question the wisdom of admitting as much.

Catherine's gaze fell to the surface of the water and he knew the moment she saw the evidence of her effect upon him. She looked at him in alarm and Rhys could not help but smile.

"You can expect little else when you surprise me in the bath, my lady."

"I see. I mean, I understand, not that I see..." She fell silent as her cheeks flushed scarlet. He was certain she would flee then, but incredibly, she remained. He could see the flutter of her pulse at her throat and heard her quick breath. Her nipples beaded before his very eyes and Rhys did not even want to blink lest he miss one detail.

"Is there a reason for your presence?" he managed to ask, his voice uncommonly hoarse.

"A kiss, sir. I would have a kiss." Her voice dropped, becoming husky and impossibly alluring. "Rhys." There it was again, his name on her lips, the most seductive sound he had ever heard. Catherine lowered her lashes, hiding her thoughts from his view, and he felt cheated.

Then she swallowed, leaned closer and touched her lips to his.

Rhys froze in shock, his grip tightening on the sides of the tub. Fire surged through him from the point of contact, launching a desire sufficient to make him roar. He held back from reciprocating, fearful of frightening her, wondering at this unexpected marvel.

He was the one who had intended to seduce her, after all.

To be sure, it was a clumsy kiss, the angle all wrong. Their teeth clicked but when Catherine might have pulled away in dismay, Rhys moved. He did not mean to let this moment end so quickly. He caught her nape in his hand, adjusted the angle of her head and slowly deepened the kiss. Her hair wound around his fingers, a tether of silk, and her lips were so soft that he wanted to feast upon her. She was warm and soft and he could smell both her skin and her arousal, which only fed his own.

Again, he expected her to flee, but Catherine was not so shy as that. It was utterly satisfactory to swallow her little gasp of surprise and feel her mouth soften against his. Her hand slid from his jaw into his own hair, then she was bracketing his face in her hands. She learned quickly, nearly devouring his mouth, hungry with a passion she had never shown him before.

Rhys knew this intimacy would lead him astray, but he could not resist her. When Catherine touched her tongue to his, he could not think beyond the glory of this kiss. He had time to think about tumbling her into the bath atop him before she abruptly stood up, leaving him lunging after her. He sat down hard and the water splashed, their gazes locked with a new intensity.

She stared at him, her breath coming quickly and her eyes alight. "I did not imagine it, then," she whispered inexplicably. She seized her robe and spun on her heel, pulling on the garment as she strode away from him. Even in her retreat, Rhys eyed the luscious curves of her bare feet and yearned.

It was not until she opened the connecting door that he understood. He had thought she meant to go to the bed or to a chair.

She could not leave him after that kiss!

"Catherine!" Rhys called after her, rising from the tub. She glanced back and her eyes widened, a reminder of both his nudity and his evident arousal. Then she fled the chamber on quick feet. Rhys swore and seized his robe. "Wait, Catherine!"

"I am late, sir. I journey to Rockmorton Fell with our hostess this morning."

Rhys did not intend to be turned aside, not now. But he heard the key turn in the lock just before his hand landed on the latch. What was this? He jiggled it, just the same. "Catherine," he said softly. "What game do you play?"

"No game, sir." She hesitated for a moment and from any other person, Rhys would have expected a falsehood to follow that pause. "Our hostess confided that she starts each day with a kiss from her husband. It seemed a commendable notion. As it seems to vex you, though, I will refrain in future."

Her voice was light and matter-of-fact, the tone she might use to inform him that she had replaced a parlor maid. Was she laughing at him? His Catherine was not flirtatious—but she had been with Montgomery the night before.

Had that kiss not set her aflame? Rhys wanted very much to know.

No, he wanted another kiss, a better and a longer one.

"Catherine!" he roared, but she ignored him.

"Forbes!" Rhys bellowed as he strove to dry himself with haste. "Where are you, man? I am late!"

Talk to her. Montgomery's counsel rang in his ears.

Rhys would kiss her first.

∼

Goodness!

Catherine was amazed by her own audacity.

She was more astonished by that kiss. How could the meeting of two mouths be so very beguiling? How could that touch set her simmering from head to toe, push every sensible thought from her mind, and tempt her to forget her obligations for the morning? It was a marvel, to be sure.

And she, so known for her reserve, had visited her husband while he was in his bath. He had been nude, although a great deal of his nudity had been hidden by the water, at least at first.

She had kissed him of her own volition.

She had looked upon him—well, just a little.

Despite the overwhelming satisfaction of the situation, she had followed the given counsel and denied him more than a short kiss.

She had also contrived a falsehood about Eurydice to explain her uncharacteristic choices.

There was yet more. The night before, she had deliberately dressed to entice her lord husband. She had been coquettish with their host, whose easy manner had made it simple for her to do so. She had been aware of Rhys' hungry gaze upon her and she had provoked his interest apurpose.

Truly, Catherine became a different woman at Rockmorton Manor. She might not have recognized her sensible self in these choices.

The most remarkable detail of all, however, was how much she liked the change. Sadly, there were no additional pages of the mysterious book to advise her.

Yet.

~

CATHERINE WAS SMILING when she descended to the hall to meet Eurydice, her step light. She was curious about the village and the apothecary, and intended to ask Eurydice in private about the source of these mysterious notes.

Perhaps Eurydice possessed the entire volume.

Perhaps Eurydice had written it.

To Catherine's surprise, Mrs. Oliver was sitting in the foyer in a hideous fur coat, so matted and long that she might have been consumed by an unkempt beast. Her hat was wrapped in so many veils that

Catherine could scarcely discern her face beneath them.

"Good morning, Mrs. Oliver. Do you mean to venture outside?"

"That I will, that I will." The old woman nodded vigorously. "Little Eurydice is feeling unwell today, but she did not wish to delay your visit to town. She asked that I accompany you instead."

"I would not so inconvenience you," Catherine said politely.

"It is no trouble." The lady heaved herself to her feet with herculean effort, then nodded with satisfaction. "I will fetch her that charm from the apothecary, as well."

"We could postpone the journey," Catherine suggested, concerned that it might be too much for the older woman.

"Nonsense! An outing will be good for you." Mrs. Oliver gave Catherine a friendly and entirely inappropriate nudge. "They say that absence makes the heart grow fonder. Let us test the truth of that!" She gave a cackle of laughter then and began to move toward the door.

Could she know about Catherine's actions of the morning?

That could not be. They could not have been overheard and even Foster did not know.

No, Mrs. Oliver must feel that some in the house were less enthused about her own presence.

Despite her apparent limitations, Mrs. Oliver moved more quickly than Catherine might have expected. Gaines opened the door with a bow and they passed into the chilly morning. A small carriage was already before the door, a footman holding the door. It looked too small for the two of them, given the older lady's size, and Catherine hesitated.

"You first, my dear," Mrs. Oliver said then smacked

her lips. "It will give the vehicle some ballast." She seemed to find this amusing.

"Catherine!" Rhys cried just when she was ducking into the carriage and she nearly hit her head in surprise.

Her normally composed and elegant husband was still shoving one arm into his coat as he strode toward the carriage with purpose. His cravat was not tied perfectly and his hair was disheveled, but the fact that he had raced after her made Catherine's heart jump.

She would have to remember the merit of interruptions.

"Mrs. Oliver," he said with a hasty bow to the older lady. "I will escort my wife to town, though I thank you for your kindness in offering to do as much."

"You will not cheat me of a visit to the apothecary, sir," the lady said, rapping her cane with insistence. "I can tell you tales of my gout that would have you declining all spirits for a year, if not more." She shook her cane at him. "You will not change my plans at whim to better suit you, sir, no matter how ancient your title might be."

Rhys glanced toward Catherine. His heated gaze made her mouth go dry as did the plea in his eyes. It would be folly to be alone with him. She would forget her every reason for leaving him—and not regret it a whit.

"You need not join us," she said with less conviction than might have once been the case. "Mrs. Oliver and I are content to visit town on our own."

"Yet I am not."

Her husband's decisive tone was delicious. Catherine sat down, thinking furiously of what she might say or do. Meanwhile, Rhys and the footman helped Mrs. Oliver into the carriage, a considerable effort, and she collapsed mightily on the seat beside

Catherine. The carriage had only one bench seat and the older lady filled more than half of it.

"There is not room in this carriage for three," Catherine said to Rhys, but he was already seating himself on her right side. She was crushed between the two of them as the footman closed the door. Mrs. Oliver was all softness and fabric, while Rhys was all muscled strength, a most distracting combination.

Mrs. Oliver elbowed her, claiming yet more of the seat as she did so. Catherine might have foregone the entire exercise, but the driver had cracked the whip and the horses were already trotting away from the house. She could feel Rhys' thigh pressed against her own and found herself flushing in memory of what she had glimpsed earlier. He held her fast against his side, keeping one arm locked around her waist. Mrs. Oliver sighed with satisfaction and braced her gloved hands on the head of her cane. She nodded at the view of the fields in fog.

Then, incredibly, she began to snore. She simply dropped off to sleep, much as she had done the night before, her chin sinking to her chest and her snores loud enough to make the windows rattle.

"You desired a kiss," Rhys murmured. "I hope you have not changed your mind." As if his voice at such proximity was not sufficiently troubling, the cursed man pressed his lips to the back of Catherine's neck. She shivered despite herself, feeling his warm breath there, knowing she could not escape his grip.

In truth, she did not really wish to.

Were it not for Mrs. Oliver, she might have surrendered to his amorous assault. She felt Rhys' lips on her earlobe and closed her eyes. She could scarce draw a breath and felt a little dizzy at his caress.

"I intend to grant you one to remember," Rhys whispered.

"This is inappropriate, sir," she whispered but her husband did not release her. Indeed, she wriggled a bit and his grip upon her only tightened. Her cheeks were hot and her heart was racing—yet they were not alone! "Rhys!" she whispered, scandalized as he lifted her onto his lap. She had her back to Mrs. Oliver and found herself lost in the glitter of his eyes.

"Yes, my Catherine," he murmured softly, melting her objections so that she could not think of a word to say. He smiled as he slid his gloved thumb across her mouth, then his hand rose to her nape. She dared not take a breath as he captured her mouth beneath his own.

The kiss was heavenly.

It was more demanding and more seductive than their wedding kiss, and even sweeter than the one they had just shared in his chamber. Slow and hot, it set her very blood to simmering. Catherine might have expected that one's desire for kisses could be sated, but her husband's demanding embrace readily convinced her otherwise. His kiss was languid and potent, and she was powerless to resist his touch. Indeed, she could not imagine why she should. She closed her eyes and kissed him back, echoing his gestures, aware of his arousal and her ability to influence it. Indeed, she loved every second of this endless kiss.

Until Mrs. Oliver harrumphed and stirred. She coughed, jabbed her elbow into Catherine's back, then rapped her cane on the roof of the carriage. "Halt, my good man. Halt!"

The carriage lurched to a stop and the older woman fell upon the latch. Catherine slid back to the seat of the carriage, feeling flustered. Rhys did not relinquish his grip upon her waist.

The footman swept open the door and bowed. "Madame?"

"I must return to the house immediately," Mrs. Oliver insisted, moving to get out of the carriage.

"Praise be," Rhys murmured.

"But we are far from the house, Mrs. Oliver," Catherine protested. "How will you manage to return there?" Rhys gave her a squeeze but she granted him an indignant look. "We cannot abandon her and she cannot walk so far."

Rhys looked resolute, as if he would gladly do as much. She was tempted to chide him mightily for his selfish disregard for the older woman.

It would have been easier if she hadn't been in instinctive agreement.

The older woman pointed down the road with her cane. "Whose carriage is that approaching?" she demanded of the footman.

"It appears to be Reverend Potter, madame. I recognize his horse."

The horse in question was a dapple with black socks, a stocky creature with a distinctive gait. The carriage proved to be an open cart, with a man seated alone within it.

"Stop him, then," Mrs. Oliver commanded. "The good parson cannot decline to deliver an old lady home." The footman stepped into the road and raised his hand.

"What of your visit to the apothecary?" Catherine asked. "What of your gout?"

Rhys inhaled slightly.

"It will not vanish anytime soon." Mrs. Oliver patted Catherine's hand. "You bring me a potion, if you please." Her eyes glinted behind the veils as she glanced toward Rhys. "If you remember. Oh, I have such a fondness for a well-sprung carriage." With an inexplicable hoot of laughter, she accepted the footman's assistance to hobble to the waiting cart.

~

MRS. OLIVER'S departing words recalled Rhys to his senses.

To be sure, he enjoyed little more than a spontaneous romp, but this was *Catherine*. While he welcomed her newfound interest in physical affection, he knew that if he overwhelmed her with sensation, she might regret her choice. She was not impulsive and not normally demonstrative, and she would not like the servants whispering about their deed.

Seduction could go badly awry, ensuring only that she later despised him.

Rhys' own enthusiasm aside, the better course would be to argue his position logically. He should discover the reason why she considered a return to her father's house, then make a case against it.

He should talk to her, as Montgomery had suggested.

Rhys placed a distance between them, willed his ardor to cede for the moment, and strove to gather his thoughts. All rode on the merit of the argument he might make.

He had mere moments to decide how best to begin.

~

INSTEAD OF ANOTHER GLORIOUS KISS, there was silence in the carriage and a decided gap between Catherine and her husband after Mrs. Oliver's departure. Catherine straightened her bonnet and arranged her skirts, still feeling disheveled when she was done. Why had Rhys not continued what they had begun? Evidently, he had reconsidered the impulsive appeal of his actions. She did not dare to look at him and see in his expression that he found her lacking.

Catherine could think of no other explanation. He could not have been pretending to find her attractive for Mrs. Oliver's benefit, and Rhys was not dishonest. He simply regretted his choice.

She should have gone with Mrs. Oliver.

"Did you truly wish her to remain?" Rhys asked finally, his voice curiously tight.

"We could not leave her in the road, sir," Catherine said crossly. "You were most unchivalrous to even suggest as much and I expected greater courtesy from you." The interior of the carriage seemed to warm and she risked a glance at her husband, only to see that he began to smile. She could not fathom why.

Nor could she avert her gaze. She felt her color rise but felt compelled to continue. "She is Montgomery's aunt and guest. It would be discourteous and is most unsuitable behavior for another guest…"

"Ah, Catherine," her husband murmured inexplicably, leaning his head back and closing his eyes. "You undermine my every good intention."

She frowned. "I cannot imagine how that might be, sir."

Rhys turned toward her, his gaze so compelling that Catherine could not take a breath. He spoke in that seductive murmur that made her forget all else in the world. "You should know, my lady, how tempted I am to be discourteous, simply to experience your outrage."

Catherine straightened and turned away. "You mock me, sir."

"I assure you that I do not." He raised a hand, as if unwillingly, and laid claim to a curl before her ear. She saw his gloved fingertip from the periphery of her vision and felt the smooth leather of his glove brush her cheek. Her heart stopped cold. She risked a sidelong glance to find him watching closely as he wrapped the tendril around his gloved finger. Catherine could neither take a breath nor pull away, especially when he swallowed visibly. "I told you that no one had chastised me before you." His gaze rose to hers, hot and intent.

"But that must be nonsense. It cannot be true that you were never reprimanded."

"Because I deserve it so much?" he asked, his tone teasing, and Catherine stammered an incoherent reply. He did not release her curl of hair. "Schoolmasters and tutors do not count, my lady."

"Your father."

He shook his head and dropped his gaze, hiding his thoughts from her. "Never stirred himself to bother."

Catherine felt sympathy for him then. "Your mother."

"Died in the delivery of me. I have no recollection of the sound of her voice."

Catherine wanted to console him, for all his light words. Her own mother had been gone only a few years and she missed her daily. "Your sisters." She knew he had possessed several, none of whom survived.

"I could do no wrong in their eyes." His sudden grin was mischievous. "How else do you think I became so in need of your scolding?"

She took a shaking breath, tearing her gaze from his mouth. "I do not scold."

"No. You are gentle but firm. Reprimand is a better choice of word. You do it admirably—as if we were each wrought for the other."

Catherine did not know what to make of that, so she stared straight ahead. "Even for its novelty, you cannot enjoy it."

"But I do." His voice dropped impossibly lower. "Those days we spend reviewing the accounts each month are the happiest I know. I look forward to them with enthusiasm, even though you often chastise me."

"Less often this past year," she felt compelled to note.

Rhys rubbed his thumb against the curl, his gaze locking again with her own. Catherine was astonished by his words and her thoughts muddled by his touch. He quirked a brow, which made him look singularly wicked. "Indeed, I have been tempted to indulge in proliferate spending on occasion, simply in anticipation of your wrath."

He *was* teasing her. She tugged her curl from his grip and stared out the window. "I believe you do mock me, sir."

"No, Catherine." Rhys shook his head, his tone as solemn as she had heard. "Have you not realized the truth of it? One only chastises when one cares." She turned to look as he swallowed, his hot gaze dropping to her lips. "And I very much like knowing that you care enough to reprimand me."

Oh.

Rhys leaned closer, the brush of his breath against her cheek making her shiver. The man could make her dizzy without even trying, and could persuade her to forget all she knew. Catherine swallowed and looked down at her hands. Would he kiss her again? Was she a fool to hope so fervently that he would?

"And that is why I cannot do what I should do."

Catherine could make no sense of these words.

But Rhys frowned and peered out the window. His mouth was a grim line and he changed the subject when he finally spoke. "Why do you even consider the possibility of returning to your father's house?"

"Because we do not truly have a marriage."

"Do we not confer together each month, united in our purpose?"

"That is only a small measure of a marriage bond."

"Are you lacking for any trinket or comfort?"

Catherine opened her mouth and closed it again. It would seem too pathetic to ask for his attention. "I would like to have a child, if not several." Did she imagine the look of revulsion that momentarily claimed his features? "You have need of an heir, sir."

He inhaled sharply. "I must confess the truth of it," he said abruptly, then turned that vivid gaze upon her. "I do not wish you to leave, Catherine, or return to your father's house." His gaze held hers with intensity as her heart skipped. "I like you."

Her hopes plummeted. This was not the confession she had hoped to hear, though she knew it was not reasonable to expect more.

Rhys continued, unaware of her dismay. "I like how you manage matters and how you are forthright and honest. I like that I can trust you completely to do what is right, even if it is difficult, even in my absence. You are an excellent partner, given your good sense. My properties have been houses and obligations, but when you are in residence, they are homes."

Catherine felt a glow of pleasure at this.

"My household have come to rely upon you for fair treatment, which is admirable. And I think you do some good for the world at large by teaching me to overcome my shortcomings." His tone was light, his gaze challenging. "As a result of what can be said to be a compelling and rational argument, I am asking you to stay."

Catherine was surprised. What had happened to his plan to seduce her? Had she been wrong to hope for it? She knew she would be susceptible to any charm that Rhys expended, but he had not troubled himself to do as much.

"I had understood, sir, that you meant to seduce me." She tried to sound formal but was sure he would hear her disappointment.

He winced but she was uncertain why. "I have thought the better of it."

"Even though Mr. Murdoch advised as much." She heard an increment of bitterness in her own words.

"It would be an inappropriate strategy, I fear, my lady." Rhys eyed her. "A woman of such good sense as yourself would not be swayed by such fleeting pleasure—or worse, she would regret her choice later. I must appeal to your practical nature and I do. Stay, Catherine, that we may continue as we have done."

His sole concern must be her fortune—and perhaps her usefulness.

At that, Catherine's composure was dismissed.

CHAPTER 5

*R*hys knew immediately that he had said the wrong thing, but it was hard to regret as much when Catherine's eyes blazed with fury. She straightened, a spot of color lighting in each cheek, and took a breath before berating him.

She was superb.

"A wife, sir, should not be merely *useful*," she said with a heat that curled his toes. "Though I am certain it is agreeable to save the funds that might be expended upon an estate manager or an accountant, there should be more to marriage that a monthly meeting about the finances. Doubtless you do not understand how convivial a union can be, given the early loss of your mother, but I was raised in a household filled with affection. My mother and father were partners in every way until her demise, and my father misses her greatly. They conferred over the accounts, to be sure, but they talked together, they laughed together, they raised my sisters and I together, and they shared tasks together. They lifted each other's spirits when the situation demanded it, they consoled each other, and they loved each other with all their hearts. Their marriage was the only example I ever knew of that union, and I could only expect the same for myself."

"But our match was arranged, my lady."

"So was theirs! Never has there been so perfect a union, though my mother told me that it was not easily won. They argued at first about their joint path and differing expectations, but they talked together. They created plans and forged a life together that gave each what he or she wanted most. They compromised. They consulted. They loved and they forgave."

Rhys was intrigued. He realized he had never seen the workings of a successful marriage himself. Even his sisters' matches had been observed from a distance—and they had been of short duration.

"You, sir, took my hand in yours for the sake of my inheritance and dowry. Now, it is clear, you would keep me by your side to ensure both the fortune in your coffers and my management of the funds. That is not a marriage as I know it. That is a business relationship. I yearn for more, sir, and my father is not a fool to say I deserve more. You grant more of your attention to your horses, and even in your stables, it is ensured that the mares breed regularly."

Rhys would have asked the obvious question, but Catherine jabbed her fingertip into his thigh.

"I always desired children, sir. I always wanted a family like my own, a house filled with love and laughter regardless of its size, a husband who cared for both wife and children regardless of his wealth or station, and a joy in marriage to be celebrated in each other's companionship each and every day, regardless of how much time my spouse and I might have together." She shook her head, her disappointment in him palpable. "No one wishes to be taken for granted. I never ever wished to be appreciated for being useful, like a favored pot in the kitchens."

"But Catherine, you came to me this morning…"

"Fool that I was, I hoped that you only needed encouragement to come to me. I thought, mistakenly, that you did not realize I would gladly meet you abed. I know little of such intimate matters, sir, but even I know that a husband must come to his wife's bed for children to be conceived. That you cannot bear to deliver the marital debt is disheartening and good cause to accept my father's suggestion. How can we make a union if you find me abhorrent?"

The carriage halted then and the footman—who might have been listening to Catherine—opened the door with cursedly efficient timing. Rhys had no chance to give his reply as his lady left the carriage.

"I will not be long," she told the footman and proceeded into the apothecary alone, spine straight and chin high, a pale statue of perfection again.

Abhorrent. She thought he found her unattractive.

That was as far from the truth as could be.

How could Rhys convince Catherine of the truth in his heart?

He got out of the carriage and surveyed the main throughway of the small village. It was quaint with timbered buildings and an excellent view of the sea. He took note of a tavern and a small emporium in addition to the apothecary, as well as signs before a number of houses, noting the specialties of local tradesmen. A few people were about their business and there were garlands of greenery hanging over the shop windows.

He was keenly aware of both footman and driver awaiting his decision. "I will walk to the harbor," he said, indicating its direction with his cane. "Pray persuade my wife to wait for my return." The footman smirked before he bowed, proof that he *had* been listening, and Rhys turned away.

He had to think of precisely what to say to apologize. He knew he would have only one chance, for Catherine was vexed.

Truth be told, her expectations from marriage sounded most promising. He had never imagined a man could gain so much from a match.

He eyed the sky and considered the magnitude of what he would lose if Catherine left him. Rhys knew his heart would never heal. He had to put aside his conviction in the curse and seduce his wife thoroughly.

It was difficult to regret the immediate implications of that course.

CATHERINE SCARCELY SAW the wonders of the apothecary, her blood was simmering with such outrage. It was a lovely establishment, neat and organized, with light flooding through the front windows. The shelves behind the counter were lined with jars of various sizes with the names of plants and potions upon them. She could see that herbs hung from the ceiling in the back room to dry and there was a pleasant scent of cinnamon and anise. There were several villagers in the shop when she arrived and the couple behind the counter served them as she tried to calm herself.

Sensible. Practical. Catherine hated having these traits presented as her assets, especially when it was Rhys who made the list. She wanted so much more.

She had to be fair, though, that her pride was injured. Rhys had only confessed this plan to seduce her when he had heard of her proposed departure—and he could not bring himself to do as much, even for the fortune at stake. Was she so plain as that?

She could change many details, but not her face.

The apothecary's wife approached and Catherine turned her attention to her errand. The charm for Eurydice had already been made, the woman having planned to send it to the house unbidden. It was made of red felt, like a gingerbread man, with red hearts embroidered upon it. Inside the stuffing, she was assured, were dried herbs of a scent that would help distract the lady from her pains in delivering the child. The apothecary's wife also recommended an herbal mixture for a tisane that would aid in recovery after the birth.

Catherine also indulged in a skin tonic for herself, then a charm for Foster to find a true love. It would be a welcome addition to the Christmas gift she had brought for the maid.

When she left with her parcel, she found Rhys awaiting her beside the carriage, his expression somber. He appeared to be subdued and she could not blame him after her tirade.

"My lady," Rhys said, tipping his hat. He offered his hand to help her into the carriage, his manners impeccable. He spoke softly when she stood beside him. "I would ask for the opportunity to argue my side, if you please."

Catherine stopped and looked up at him, ashamed that she had been so vehement. Had she injured his feelings? "I apologize for my outburst, sir."

His smile warmed her heart. "I undoubtedly deserved no less." He kissed her knuckles, the glint in his eyes making her knees weak. "It is appalling that I should leave you with the impression that you have the merit of a kitchen pot, as reliably useful as such an item may be. You are a treasure, Catherine, and I owe you an explanation, if you will indulge me."

"I will," she said, intrigued.

They were well on the way to Rockmorton Manor when Rhys finally spoke. To Catherine's surprise, he had laid claim to her hand and held it captive upon his thigh. "The simple fact of it is that I do not want you to leave, Catherine, and it is not because of whatever funds might follow you. I admire your notion of how a marriage should be and I apologize that I know so little of such unions. I greatly appreciate your explanation." His smile was wry. "It appears that you will have to tutor me in this matter, as well."

"I have only my family's example to follow."

"And it is a good one. I would ask you to grant our match a second chance and a fresh opportunity. I apologize for my errors of these past years. I ask for your trust in accepting that I had good cause in keeping my distance, but in future I will strive to do as you ask." He smiled. "I will mend my ways, in the interest of compromise, which you so eloquently defended."

"I would not place a burden upon you, sir," she began but Rhys silenced her with a fleeting kiss, one that made her eyes widen.

"You mistake the matter if you believe I find your presence merely convenient," he whispered, remaining close. Her hands were captive within his own and his gaze bored into hers. "You are the most alluring lady of my acquaintance, Catherine."

How she yearned to believe him, but did she dare? She dropped her gaze.

"If you are willing to try to conceive an heir for Trevelaine, I am your servant."

Catherine turned to him, knowing her surprise showed. "Even though I am plain?"

"Plain?" His distaste was clear. "Who told you such a lie, Catherine?"

"I thought you did not find me pleasing. I thought that was why…"

His thumb landed over her lips, silencing her in a most pleasant way, and his gaze bored into hers. "You are wrong," he said with vehemence and again, she thought he might kiss her.

But Rhys drew back with obvious reluctance. "I must recall my obligations as a gentleman," he said tightly. "In respect of the decision you must make, I will not come to you on this night or any other without an invitation." He shot her a glance that was all green fire. He felt strongly about the matter, whatever the cause. Catherine knew what she wanted it to be. "I do not want you to regret a choice in my favor, though I will do my utmost to ensure that you do not. Choose, Catherine, and I will abide by your decision. It goes without saying that I hope you will choose our marriage."

He could have overwhelmed her objections with a touch and Rhys knew it as well as Catherine. In a way she appreciated that he did not try.

In another, she regretted it.

But he understood her well enough to understand that only a choice based upon clear thinking would satisfy her in the end.

How curious that she would wish, just a little, to be swept away by his passion, even to make a choice she might later regret. How unlike the sensible woman she knew herself to be.

Would Rhys ever cease to challenge her expectations?

What should she do?

THEY RODE the rest of the way in silence, and Rhys departed for the stables after he had handed Catherine out of the carriage. She watched him go, torn between her choices.

Fortunately, there was no sign of either the reverend or Mrs. Oliver once she entered the house. She spent the remainder of the day with Eurydice, who confessed to feeling much better. Catherine had not been able to engage as much as usual in their lively discussion about books, not with her thoughts so distracted by Rhys.

An unexpected snow began to fall late that afternoon. Eurydice and Catherine stood at the window watching it steadily cover the ground with a blanket of white. The sky was a dull grey overhead and there was not a breath of wind. Every creature seemed to have taken shelter and the only movement was the swirling of the snow. It was so peaceful.

"I have never seen such snow," Catherine confessed, fascinated. "It falls so softly that it is surprising to see how much it has accumulated."

"There is something relentless about it," Eurydice agreed, untroubled. "It often snows at my sister's home in Scotland and you should know that we have provisions for a good many days." Her hostess was peering once again into Catherine's satchel of unread books. "It is a marvel that so many people write books."

"No less that so many of them are terrible," Catherine said and they laughed together.

"Mine is not a terrible book."

Catherine turned at her friend's resolute tone. "You are writing a book?" She was sure that Eurydice would confess to writing the guide from which she had read excerpts.

But she was mistaken.

"It is a novel in three volumes," Eurydice confessed with enthusiasm. "It is almost completed. It would have been finished by now, if not for my husband's tendency to interrupt." She flushed and dropped a hand to her stomach. "Although I cannot truly complain of that."

Then what was the source of the passages left in her room. Catherine might have asked, but she had no opportunity.

Eurydice cleared her throat. "I do not wish to impose, but I wondered whether you might read my book so far. I would appreciate an objective opinion, particularly from someone who knows so much about fiction."

"Of course. I would be delighted."

Eurydice was watching her. "I feared that you had not offered because you would prefer not to read the work of a friend."

Catherine went to her side immediately. "I confess that I have been distracted. I am sorry."

"You should not be. I should complete it before you return to London and will give it to you then."

"I thank you for your trust." The two women smiled at each other, then Eurydice glanced toward the satchel.

"Is there another one of merit?"

Catherine donned her glasses and retrieved a manuscript. "I thought the beginning of this one had promise," she said and placed it into Eurydice's eager hands.

"A ghost, a curse and an abandoned castle. How marvelous!" Her friend settled by the fire, her anticipation obvious.

When Catherine glanced down, she saw the note in the satchel.

It was another excerpt.

Catherine glanced at Eurydice, who was absorbed in her book, then read it.

Upon the merit of blunt speech at rare intervals...

It is an unfortunate truth that even the most wondrous of gentlemen may on occasion speak or act in a way that is hurtful to a lady. It is this writer's view that no lady should ever have to accommodate herself to such injustices and that the interjection of a timely word can ensure that such circumstances are not repeated, much less become habitual.

This is not to suggest that a gentleman should be harangued or threatened. A lady may however take issue with oversights, harsh words undeserved, neglected manners, forgotten obligations and/or broken promises, among other situations that should not be endured.

It is also recommended to conclude any such discussion with a solution of choice. This ensures that the gentleman can take ready action to repair whatever damage has been done. Words and actions are more compelling than gems, and requesting them will never give the impression that a lady is avaricious. A sincere apology is invariably a fine choice, and perhaps a gesture of goodwill to buttress the apology. The more precisely the lady can define what she would deem suitable to set all aright again, the better her likelihood of success.

One must also recall that to err is human and to forgive, divine...

How curious that the timing of these excerpts was so excellent. It was almost as if someone—undoubtedly the author of *The Ladies' Essential Guide*—knew of Catherine's situation and was urging her to resolve it.

Eurydice glanced up then, her brows rising as her gaze lit on the sheet.

"I thought perhaps this was your book," Catherine said.

"It would be a very short one."

Catherine smiled. "I have discovered a number of these excerpts. There obviously is a complete work somewhere."

"Is it good?"

"It is very interesting." She handed the page to Eurydice, then perched on a chair waiting for her opinion.

Eurydice's lips formed a little o of surprise. "Oh!" she said, then obviously read it again. She met Catherine's gaze. "How forthright. Is it all like this?"

"Some pages are more so."

"A guide for ladies that tells the truth. How innovative," Eurydice's smile turned wicked. "Perhaps you should encourage your father to publish it. It might become a sensation."

Catherine had little doubt of that. "It is not your work, though?"

Eurydice shook her head. "I should never be so bold."

"Then whose might it be?"

"I cannot imagine." Eurydice shrugged, her attention straying to the manuscript she held. "You are right. The beginning of this one is most promising. Forgive me if I must continue reading."

"Of course." Catherine retrieved the excerpt and read it again, then rose to watch the snow again as she thought about Rhys. She had to admit she had not been entirely fair.

The comparison to her parents' marriage was a telling one. She and Rhys did work together when it came to the management of funds, much as her parents had done. Advised of her concerns, he had adapted his ways and curtailed his expenses. He had acted upon her suggestions to better align expenses and income at both properties, and had been remarkably accommodating.

It was as if he had been simply waiting for good counsel—and he recognized it when he found it. He had changed from the man she had married. Rhys no longer spent absurd quantities of coin. (She remembered being shocked by how much he had spent at bootmakers.) He no longer was impulsive in dispensing funds and the whim to grant generous gifts was evidently banished. When he wished to make a large expenditure, he discussed the details with her. The new carriage was a perfect example. He had come to their monthly meeting with an accounting of what he thought was required in a new carriage and why, then several estimates from carriagemakers and their various reputations. They had conferred and made the choice together.

Indeed, those meetings were more than convivial. Catherine looked forward to them every month and had noted more than once the contrast between her husband's appearance of indifference and when he was paying keen attention.

He liked her.

That confession made her heart glow, for she liked him, too. He made her laugh at least once during each monthly encounter, and listened to her arguments with attention. He never dismissed her concerns though they had once argued the merit of a more expensive option over a cheaper one. He spoke to her as an equal when they did speak and he treated her as a person of intellect and merit.

What example of marriage was within his experience? His mother had died in childbirth so he had never witnessed his parents' marriage. A man could not be blamed for failing to know something he had never been taught or had the opportunity to learn.

Further, though she had heard all the rumors of Rhys' wild ways, Catherine had no evidence they continued. There was no sign that he kept a mistress and if he gambled, he must have experienced a long winning streak since their wedding day. She would have noticed the disappearance of funds or heard of any debts.

Perhaps her marriage made greater progress toward the union she desired than she had realized.

She knew it would be madness to abandon what she had in hope of romance. No, the sensible solution was to continue to build upon success.

Catherine folded the missive, her decision made. How fortunate that she had heeded the suggestion of that dressmaker, the one who was evidently in vehement agreement with Rhys. Her younger sister had insisted that the dressmaker was right about the color and Catherine, though unconvinced, had ceded.

But she had a red dress of precisely the same garnet hue as the shawl Rhys had given to her. Wearing that to dinner could leave no doubt that he would attend her words.

The Ladies' Essential Guide to the Art of Seduction had taught her that.

~

RHYS SPENT the day in agitation. He rode out with Montgomery and discussed the merit of various horses and dogs, but his concern was entirely upon Catherine. The two men considered the falling snow together and Montgomery reviewed the preparations for a storm, which Rhys scarcely heeded.

When he dressed for dinner, he was tempted to tap upon his wife's door, but he forestalled the impulse.

He would not press Catherine. Rhys wasn't a patient man but he was determined to be so in this matter. He would even endure Mrs. Oliver's noisy consumption of her sherry with good humor.

But Rhys did not have to be patient for long. As soon as he heard Catherine's step upon the stairs and pivoted to look, he knew. His heart pounded and a warmth suffused him at the sight of her. Catherine wore a dress he had never seen before, a glorious crimson garment that favored her coloring perfectly. It was the same shade as the shawl he had given to her, which she also carried. She wore the pearls she had worn for her marriage—her mother's, he recalled—and had abandoned her glasses. Her hair was in the same soft arrangement as the night before, and he admired how the golden curls brushed against her nape.

He met her at the bottom of the stairs, her smile and

the sparkle in her eyes telling him all he needed to know. "Splendid," he said with approval, casting a glance over her. "It seems you do not need my assistance at the dressmaker, for I could not have chosen better."

"Patricia argued your case in your absence, without even knowing of it."

Rhys laughed at this mention of her younger sister. "I hope you have your glasses in your reticule. One must be certain of what one consumes."

She laughed and withdrew them with reluctance.

"I think they suit you," he said, meaning every word and her smile as she donned them made his heart light. "Dare I hope you have made a choice?"

Catherine sobered. "I must have a true marriage, Rhys, in every way, or I would rather have none at all." Her gaze was searching, her uncertainty of him sufficient to tear at his heart.

Children were the condition of her remaining with him.

The curse must be ignored.

Rhys took a steadying breath, knowing she could walk away from him this very moment if he declined.

He nodded once and saw relief light her smile. "May I come to you tonight?" he asked softly and felt her shiver in anticipation.

"Tonight," Catherine agreed to his relief and he kissed the back of her hand.

The meal could not progress quickly enough to suit Rhys.

RHYS WAS oblivious to Montgomery's conversation and even the taste of his friend's brandy. He abandoned his glass without finishing it to join the ladies. Eurydice was singing at the pianoforte, and although she did not have a spectacular voice, she made up for the deficit with her enjoyment of playing. Catherine, quite predictably, was reading a book but she looked up with a smile at his appearance.

It seemed an eternity before the entire company retired. Montgomery kissed his wife beneath the mistletoe and Rhys seized the opportunity to do the same. He was not prepared for Catherine to fairly melt against him, urging him to deepen his embrace. It was all too easy to surrender to the pleasure of her touch, to hold her close and to imagine the pleasures of the night ahead.

Then Mrs. Oliver rapped her cane. "You have private chambers, sir. Pray do not compel all of us to share the sight of your intimacies."

Rhys lifted his head to find Montgomery grinning and Catherine flushing. "I beg you not to linger overlong, sir," she whispered, a merry twinkle in her eyes. She then climbed the stairs with Eurydice and the odious Mrs. Oliver. Catherine glanced back once from the summit and blew Rhys a kiss, a welcoming indication that set his very blood afire.

Once again, he was caught between immediate desire and his fear for the future.

He could and would fulfill her request.

And he would do it this very night.

CATHERINE COULD NOT BEAR the waiting. She heard Rhys enter his chamber and the low murmur of his discussion with Forbes. She was in that silk dressing gown, sitting on the side of her bed, cold with anticipation. Her heart was thundering but it skipped a beat when there was a tap upon the connecting door.

"Enter," she managed to say and Rhys stepped into her chamber with the ease of a man who visited her all the time. He smiled and she stood up, uncertain how to proceed.

But he knew, of course, and he made it easy for her.

Rhys halted before her and framed her face in his hands, bending slowly to capture her lips beneath his own. His kiss was sweet and gentle, as if he asked her permission to continue. Despite the thunder of her pulse, Catherine kissed him back, her heart warming with gratitude.

In this matter, he was her tutor and she trusted him. The kiss went on, as if he had no intention of ending it. His fingers were in her hair and she leaned against his chest, her hands touching his bare skin. He angled his mouth over hers, deepening their kiss, and she mimicked his movements, sliding her mouth over his, learning to use her lips and teeth and tongue to conjure pleasure. She felt his fingers move in her hair and dared to slide her own beneath his robe, caressing the smooth warmth of his skin. His body was firmer than her own, all smooth strength and power, and she ran her hand down the tangle of hair on his chest. Rhys caught his breath when her fingertips found his flat nipple and she might have pulled away, but he placed his hand over hers.

"It is a wise choice for you to explore," he murmured. He stepped away then to extinguish the lamps, leaving only the fire glowing in the grate and the white radiance of the snow beyond the windows. He beckoned to her and she joined him before the crackling fire, watching as it put golden lights in his hair. When she stood before him, he shed his robe, casting it across a chair and baring himself to her view. Rhys lifted his hands, inviting her survey, and Catherine looked.

More, she touched. His shoulders were broad and

his skin a pale gold even in this season. She ran her fingertips across his back then down his spine to his tight buttocks. His thighs were powerful and she let her fingertips slide over his hips. When he turned to face her, she did not dare to look down, but fixed her gaze upon his face.

Rhys smiled and guided her hands back to his nipples. He showed her, one hand over her own, how to tease the nipple to a point, the sharpening of his gaze revealing that he liked it. On impulse, she bent and touched the peak with her lips, bestowing a kiss upon it, and smiled when he caught his breath. She ran her hands across his chest, then held his gaze as she let them slide every lower. He was so trim, so powerful, that she was in awe of the differences between their bodies.

"Look," he urged in a whisper and she did, not having expected the dimensions of him. He guided her hand to surround him and she saw his jaw clench when she caressed him.

She was not without power in this exchange and that emboldened her beyond all else.

"Fair is fair," he noted in that velvety low voice and Catherine unfastened her own robe. She had chosen the azure silk one and her hair was unbound. She was not prepared for the sight of Rhys' agitation when she let the robe fall. There was wonder in his eyes and that part of him clearly indicated his enthusiasm.

He turned her in front of him, his fingertips sliding across her skin much as hers had touched his. When she faced him again, there was less space between them and her breast was cupped in his palm. He slid his thumb across the nipple and it tightened to a peak, then he bent to kiss it and she gasped at the surge of pleasure emanating from that point. Then Rhys' arm was around her waist, drawing her against his hard strength, and

Catherine closed her eyes in delight. His mouth closed over hers in a kiss more demanding than any other had been thus far, and she shivered when his hand slid down her belly to her thighs.

She remembered this part and the pleasure he had kindled with his touch. She wrapped her arms around him and kissed him back, surrendering completely as he lowered her to the thick Persian rug and pleasured her as he had once before.

It was even more heavenly the second time.

HOURS LATER, Rhys watched Catherine sleep. He had touched her and savored her release, then pleasured her again. When she had collapsed against him, he had carried her back to her bed. It had not taken long for her to doze off, though he would not sleep soon. He was raging with need—he could have taken her, but in the last moment, he had been unable to do it.

So he lay beside her and touched himself, aroused by the sight of her in repose, the delicate flush upon her cheeks, the softness of her mouth, the ache in his heart that he loved her beyond all else—yet knowing that he willingly deceived her.

But Rhys could not put his beloved at risk.

CHAPTER 6

*C*atherine awakened in the morning and smiled at the flood of contentment in her heart. Rhys was beside her but sound asleep, his hair tousled and his body warm. She dared to snuggle against him and he cast an arm around her waist without waking.

She might have stayed there for hours, if another note had not been slipped beneath her door. She saw the white corner of it emerge into the room and heard the slide of it across the floor.

What did it say?

She eased from the bed without awakening Rhys, found her glasses and read the note.

Upon conception.

Whether a lady desires to conceive or wishes to avoid that situation, an understanding of the timing of such a process is most useful. When a lady experiences her courses on a regular basis, the dates of her fertility can be calculated quite readily...

Catherine read the details, then calculated the matter for herself. She smiled as she glanced toward Rhys. The ideal day, according to this counsel, would be

Christmas Day itself. It was the 22nd. Rhys stirred and she might have shared the happy news, but a woman's scream rent the air.

Eurydice!

Catherine seized her robe and opened the door even as Rhys sat up nude in her bed.

"Eurydice!" Montgomery declared as he ran to the stairs. "It is her time! Where is the midwife? Where is Gaines? Hurry, all of you, it is *time*! And the snow! Why does it have to fall today? How will the midwife get here?" He lunged down the stairs in a blind panic, oblivious to any response.

Foster was coming down the hall with her breakfast tray. Catherine decided she would dress and go to Eurydice, in case she could be of assistance. It would be her first time witnessing a birth and she was curious beyond all.

There was no sign of Rhys and the adjoining door was securely closed. Perhaps he guessed her intention and preferred to avoid such concerns of women.

Perhaps he could distract Montgomery.

Their host was shouting in the foyer and Catherine smiled at his agitation.

Perhaps Montgomery could not be distracted before the babe safely arrived.

IF RHYS NEEDED a reminder of the peril that faced Catherine if he consummated their match, he could not have found a better one. Eurydice had a long labor, one that left him tearing at his hair as much as Montgomery. The two of them watched the snow and made a tremendous amount of brandy disappear over the first day and night. On the afternoon of the second day,

Montgomery was summoned from the terse silence of the library and Rhys feared the worst.

He would never know Catherine. He would cherish her and give her anything she requested, he would entreat her to stay, but he would never go to her bed again.

It was the only safe choice.

~

ON THE AFTERNOON of December 24, the baby deigned to arrive.

After the duration of Eurydice's labor, Catherine felt her tears rise at the sound of the baby's first cry. She had remained with Eurydice the entire time and was tired beyond all, though she had only watched, talked to Eurydice and bathed her brow. She could not begin to imagine her friend's exhaustion. The charm had been clutched with such vigor that it was a shadow of its former self.

The midwife cleaned the babe as Catherine watched, awed by the perfection of his tiny hands and feet. He grimaced and began to cry in earnest, his face turning ruddy as he howled. He had a sprinkling of dark hair on his head and she had already seen that his eyes were blue.

"A boy!" Montgomery cried and kissed Eurydice soundly. "You are a marvel," he whispered, such heat in his voice that Eurydice flushed and Catherine averted her gaze, a lump in her throat. She could not wait until she and Rhys shared a similar joy.

The countess leaned back on the pillows in relief as her husband raced from the chamber. Catherine heard Montgomery shout the tidings from the top of the stairs and the cheers from the servants that followed. Where was Rhys? In such a moment, she wanted to curl against him and talk of the future, what names they would choose for their sons, and more. She ached that she had not seen him in almost two days.

Catherine surrendered the swaddled and washed child to Montgomery on his return, blinking back tears at the marvel of it all. The two women smiled at each other and the midwife fussed around the bed.

Montgomery rocked his son and cooed to him, taking him to the window. The boy ceased his cries at the low sounds of his father's voice. "Welcome to Rockmorton Manor," Montgomery said. He angled the infant to give him a better view out the window and Catherine smiled at the pride in his gesture. There was only the white of falling snow to be seen, but Montgomery was oblivious. "This will be all yours, but not soon. Your mother and I must have many more children to keep you company."

"Do not speak of that as yet," Eurydice complained cheerfully. "Grant me one night's sleep first."

"As many as you wish," Montgomery declared and returned to sit alongside her as he admired his son. Eurydice pressed a kiss to the boy's head as she studied the infant. "He is perfect and you are more so."

Catherine turned away, her throat tight.

"Nathaniel," Eurydice said, taking the baby's hand. "That must be his name."

"He has to have my father's name, as well."

"But Nathaniel first," the lady insisted. "You allowed me the choice, sir, and Charles is a forgettable name. Look upon him. He needs a name with more dignity, and I have been thinking upon it."

"You had a girl's name chosen, as well?"

"Of course!"

"What was it?"

Eurydice laughed. "I will tell you when we have a

daughter," she said and Montgomery did not seem to mind. He rocked their son.

"Nathaniel Charles Montgomery," he said and the baby made a gurgling sound. "He likes it!"

"On the contrary, he wants the breast, my lord, but does not know it yet," the midwife said and reached for the child.

"I want to try," Eurydice insisted, taking the baby to her own breast.

The midwife froze, startled. "But my lady, all the countesses of Rockmorton have had a wet nurse. I located a suitable young woman in the village just this past week..."

"My wife says she will try," Montgomery said firmly and the midwife bowed her head.

"As you wish, my lord."

Catherine knew it was common for aristocratic ladies to hire a wetnurse, but her mother had nursed all three of her daughters. Eurydice had peppered her with questions, obviously having a scheme of her own, and Catherine liked that Montgomery supported her choice. She watched as Eurydice endeavored to see the feat done, then the midwife stepped forward to counsel her. Montgomery did not move away, despite the midwife's sidelong glances of disapproval, and Catherine left the new family to their privacy.

Would Rhys support her choice to nurse their children? She rather thought he would. They would name their sons together, though. She would not dream of claiming such an important choice herself. She headed for her room, wondering whether she might be with child already and wanted to hum a tune. She could think of nothing better than Rhys in her bed each night and half a dozen children in their home.

Mrs. Oliver was making her way up the stairs, an endeavor that did not look easy, and Catherine moved to offer assistance. "A boy is it, then?" The older lady huffed as she reached the summit of the stairs.

"It is. Nathaniel."

"A good name," Mrs. Oliver said with a grunt of approval, then peered at Catherine, eyes glinting. "Your first time witnessing a birth?"

"Yes, but however did you guess?"

The older woman cackled. "There is a pallor about you that hinted at the truth. It is shocking to witness the emergence of a child, though the deed that puts it in the womb can be a pleasing affair."

Catherine frowned. She recalled what she and Rhys had done, but could not see how a child would be created in her womb as a result.

"You look bewildered, my lady," Mrs. Oliver noted.

Catherine found herself flushing. "Would it be unseemly, Mrs. Oliver, for me to ask you a question about matters of intimacy?"

"It might be, but I will not be offended." The older woman braced her hands on her cane, her manner expectant.

Catherine's cheeks burned but she had to ask. There was no one else in the corridor and no one likely to hear, but still she whispered. "How is the child conceived in the womb? What places it there?"

Mrs. Oliver inhaled sharply and Catherine thought she even growled in annoyance beneath her breath. Montgomery's aunt muttered something unintelligible and pivoted with remarkable speed, heading back toward the stairs with purpose. She thumped her way down to the foyer as Gaines looked on with astonishment, then led Catherine to the library. The older woman was breathing heavily when she halted before a shelf, peering at the titles. She pointed with her cane to a volume bound in blue leather, on a shelf above her head.

"There," she said, and the single word was sufficient for a command.

Catherine retrieved the book and handed it to her.

Mrs. Oliver dropped into a chair and fanned through the book. When she found what she sought, she handed the book to Catherine, her finger wedged between the pages. "It behooves a lady to know the mechanics of intimacy," she said, sounding so much like the pages left in her chamber that Catherine guessed their author in that instant. "I might read this in privacy, if I were you."

Montgomery appeared in the doorway in that moment, a dusty bottle in his grasp and his face still alight. "Here you are! This port was put aside by my parents on their wedding day. I propose to open it in celebration."

"Hear, hear," Mrs. Oliver said and smacked her lips. "Do not linger about the task, my boy."

But Catherine did not wish a glass of port. She had to read the book. She made her excuses, insisting that she had to change, and retreated with haste.

Once in her room, she sank to the window seat to watch the snow fall steadily, noting how it had obscured her view of the stables. It piled on the roof and sills, buried the garden and blew against the windows. Even the pathways had become difficult to discern as it swirled endlessly.

It seemed likely that Mrs. Oliver had written those excerpts. A woman who had buried three husbands would have such expertise to share, but why had she chosen to share it with Catherine?

She would have to ask her later.

Catherine took a breath and opened the book. Mrs. Oliver had opened it at the beginning of a chapter, one called *On Coitus*. The book was clearly a medical text, for she fanned through it and noted the drawings. She knew what coitus was and knew she had experienced it now. Why would Mrs. Oliver doubt her understanding?

The answer soon became clear. Catherine frowned at the unfamiliarity of the act described in the book. No part of Rhys had ever *penetrated* her. There had been no spilling of seed within her, this she knew without doubt, though she now knew why there had been wetness. The chapter continued, describing how that very liquid was necessary to conception and that the location of its deposit was critical.

Catherine stared blindly out the window at the snow.

No. If this was true, then…

She read the chapter again, her fury rising. Rhys had deceived her! Their match was not consummated at all!

Catherine slammed the book closed when she heard her husband's voice beyond the connecting door. She glared at the door, simmering, until she heard Forbes' departure. Then, caring little for her own current state of disarray, she marched to the door and tore it open. Rhys spun at the sound and he smiled in welcome, a sight that nearly undermined her resolve. But Catherine inhaled sharply and strode toward him, loosing her wrath in a torrent at the man who best deserved it.

"Sir! You deliberately deceived me!"

THEY WERE NOT the words Rhys wanted to hear when Catherine invited herself into his chamber. He had dared to be optimistic at her appearance, and truly he was relieved that Montgomery had both an heir and his wife. It was a matter to celebrate, to be sure, and his thoughts had progressed in a predictable direction when Catherine abruptly appeared.

Woe to him and his resolve that she was vexed, for she was a glorious vision, eyes snapping like fiery sapphires and cheeks flushed. Tendrils of her hair had become loose during the long day and the midwife's spare apron had not kept her dress from becoming soiled. But his heart roared that she was his wife and that she came to him, regardless of her reason.

He could entirely forget his principles beneath such an assault.

She halted before him and held his gaze, her own shining, then jabbed a finger into his chest. "You lied, sir, and you know it well. You deliberately tricked me and there is no explanation you might offer that could diminish or even temper my disappointment in your choice."

"But..."

Catherine's words swept on. "You should know that my decision is made as a result of your choice. I will be gone from Trevelaine House before your return." She was fighting tears and Rhys felt a cur of the lowest order when the first one fell. She dashed at them with her fingertips and continued to glare at him. "Did you laugh that I was fool enough to believe you?"

"No, Catherine, never." He seized her hand, knowing he would have only one chance to make amends.

"I know you despise me, but this is a cruel trick, sir. Even my family's source of wealth does not deserve such cruelty..."

"I did not intend to be cruel," he said softly.

"And yet you are." She tore her hand away from his grip. "You could have simply let me leave. You did not have to trick me. And I...I believed you," she whispered and her voice broke. "Despite my father's insistence that I was uncommonly clever. Not in your presence, to be sure." She pivoted then to leave and

Rhys knew he would never see her again if she left him now.

"It was because I love you," he said, feeling a tide of relief to have made the confession.

Catherine halted but did not turn.

Rhys had a chance.

"More lies will not make amends, sir." Her words were tight and he dared to hope that she cared, just a little.

"But this is not a lie, Catherine." Rhys dared to go to her, placing his hand upon her shoulder and turning her to face him. Her expression was anguished, a mixture of hurt and hope that tore at his heart. "I love you," he said again, holding her gaze steadily. "And thus I could not consummate our match."

"You speak nonsense, sir," she charged in a whisper.

Rhys bowed his head, keeping his hands upon her shoulders. He could feel her trembling in his grasp and he was keenly aware that the most precious element of his life be lost to him forever if he erred now. "Do you remember our wedding day?"

"It was only two years ago. I am unlikely to have forgotten it."

"Do you recall that you smiled at me, once you had made your vows?"

She shook her head, frowning slightly.

"I thought you so formal and stiff, a statue of a maiden come to put your hand in mine. I thought you dispassionate and as unlike me as could be imagined. I dreaded our future together."

"All this from a glimpse," she said quietly.

"Perhaps I looked for fault." Rhys held her gaze. "But when you completed your vows, Catherine, you smiled in your relief. I realized that you had been fearful of making an error before those gathered to witness the exchange of our vows." He smiled at her. "And that smile captured my heart. You were no icy maiden devoid of warmth and feeling, but a woman compelled into a situation that was not of her choosing. I wanted then to be the best possible husband to you, that you might find yourself rewarded for doing your duty."

"You went to your club, immediately after the wedding breakfast," she said, heat thrumming beneath her words. "That is not the choice of a man intent upon a good marriage."

"Is it not? Recognize, Catherine, that I had spent years caring only for my own whim. That you could change my view, with just one smile, was a troubling situation." He touched her lip with his fingertip and she did not move away. "I wanted to protect you. I wanted to be a good husband. I wanted to fulfill your every dream."

"To care for another was a troubling prospect?"

"To care for my wife would be to place that lady in peril."

Catherine shook her head, uncomprehending, and he led her to the fireplace. There was a blaze there, and he seated her in the biggest chair, drawing up an ottoman to sit at her feet. He rubbed her cold hands and did not release them, his fingertip returning repeatedly to the ring he had placed on her finger.

"Did no one ever warn you of my family curse?"

"Mrs. Grieves told me to give it no credence, but she did not tell me what it was."

"Did you not ask?"

Catherine caught her breath. "It seems to me that Mrs. Grieves is a person who likes to know a great many things. I chose not to reveal my ignorance to her."

Rhys laughed. "You are sensible beyond all others, my Catherine."

He felt her start, but did not let her pull her hand away. "I mean no affront. She is very capable..."

"I understand your meaning." He gently squeezed her fingers. "All the same, I do not wish to speak of Mrs. Grieves in this moment. The telling of this tale is long overdue." Rhys frowned and cleared his throat. "I am the youngest of four children and there was a formidable gap in our ages. My oldest sister, Gwendolyn, was fifteen when I was born. Penelope was thirteen and Ariana was ten. Years later, Gwendolyn confided to me that my mother had not expected to conceive again and that my father had professed himself to be content with three daughters. All the same, when my mother did find herself with child again, Gwendolyn said they were both joyous. She recalled those days of my mother's confinement as the happiest our household had ever known."

"Why did your sister tell you of this and not your father?" Catherine asked, but Rhys raised a finger to continue the tale in his own way.

"I only knew my father as a morose man, who remained alone in his library, brooding. He was not unkind, but he was by and large indifferent to everything other than his grief. My parents had a love match of uncommon power, and when my mother died in the birthing of me, I believe he wished he had died as well."

"Oh!" Catherine whispered. "I am sorry." Her fingers tightened on his for a moment. It said much of the goodness of her nature that she could forget her justified anger to console him.

"Gwendolyn might have been my mother. She taught me so much and ensured I had the right tutors. She insisted that my father send me to school, when he would not have bothered."

"He could not have blamed you for his loss."

"No, he simply no longer cared about practical matters." Rhys shook his head. "The world without my mother was to be endured."

Catherine nodded and bit her lip, her gaze fixed upon him as she listened.

"I was summoned home from school when I was twelve. My father was dying and wished to speak to me. You must realize that it was one of a very few times that he had addressed me directly or even acknowledged my presence." Rhys swallowed. "It was a daunting experience to have his undivided attention, even for those moments. He insisted that I make him a promise, and, as he was on his deathbed, he declared I would have to keep my vow. Mr. Murdoch was there, and looked much the same as he does now."

When he fell silent, Catherine put her hand over his. "What promise did he demand of you?"

Rhys met her gaze. "That I never wed for love." She caught her breath and her eyes widened, their blue hue darker than usual. "Indeed, he insisted that I should guard against loving my wife at all, for that would interfere in the provision of an heir."

Catherine was visibly confused. "I do not understand."

"He wished for me to be spared his grief."

She frowned. "I still…"

Rhys silenced her with a fingertip set against her lips. "My father explained the curse upon our family, that all beloved Bettencourt women die when delivering of an heir, whether they be daughters of the house or the wives of sons. He had not believed it himself, not until my mother died, and he blamed himself for her loss."

Catherine shook her head. "But that is irrational."

"So I thought, despite my mother's demise. But I gave him my word and he died shortly thereafter, content. I returned to school in possession of my title and inheritance. It is a curious thing to be young and know that one is wealthy. I indulged my whims, having never learned to manage coin to advantage."

Catherine's expression become prim. "I believe your estate manager exploited that situation to his own advantage."

"Indeed, and that would have continued until I was destitute if not for your keen wits." Rhys smiled at her and she blinked as if dazzled. He could only hope she found his tale persuasive. "My sisters shared in that bounty. Ariana had the most wonderful season. My other sisters were out already, but I spared no expense for Ariana's debut. She was so pretty and such delightful company. She could dance all night, every night. I knew she would make a good match if given the opportunity, and she did."

"You were a good brother, then."

"But she died in childbirth, a mere ten months after her nuptials." Rhys flicked her a hot glance. "It was a boy."

Catherine's lips parted in horror. "I am sorry," she whispered and he saw that she began to understand.

"Next, Penelope wed. Another joyous day but one that gave me some trepidation." Rhys paused and frowned. "A year later, she died in childbirth."

"Still," Catherine protested.

"Pierpont never married again, so devastated was he by Penelope's loss." He heaved a sigh. "I understand the boy excels in his lessons."

"You do not see him?" He heard Catherine's dismay. "He is your nephew!"

"He is said to favor Penelope most strongly."

"Rhys," Catherine whispered, her hands gripping his.

Rhys could not halt his tale now, not before Catherine knew it all. "Then Gwendolyn." He had to pause before he could continue. "She said she would never wed, for she wished only to know love. I was prepared to have her live in my house for the duration."

"You would have given her anything," she guessed.

"Anything," Rhys agreed heatedly. "Her marriage to Lawrence Bessborough gave her such joy, unexpected as their love was."

"You said she was fifteen years older than you. Perhaps love is more precious when it blooms late, like an autumn rose."

"Perhaps. She was thirty-four when she died in childbirth." He shook his head. "You cannot blame me for concluding that the curse is true."

Catherine sat back. "That was why you never wed."

He stared into the fire, knowing a confession was due. The words, though, did not come.

"And that was why you wed me," she said softly. "I thought it was only because the duke granted you no choice, but you wished to wed a lady you did not love."

"The duke was insistent, to be sure, but at the time I thought the solution ideal." He spared her a sad smile. "I was convinced that I could never care for a woman whose family had earned their fortune in trade."

Catherine lowered her gaze and Rhys hated that he had ever been so shallow.

"Yet I was mistaken," he added softly and she looked up with hope in her eyes. "I will not risk you, Catherine," he added with heat. "I cannot risk you. I knew it at our wedding, when you surrendered that smile, and that is why I went to my club. I knew it when you berated me for the sorry state of my accounts, so articulate and correct and concerned for our future. I knew you were the woman who would claim my heart, the only one I would treasure, and that meant I could not risk you, even for the sake of an heir."

"But your holdings..."

"I have given instruction for it all to be divided between my two nephews if I do not have one of my own. Gwendolyn's son will be granted the title."

Catherine was shaking her head. "But you are always elsewhere."

"I have been searching all my life without knowing what I sought. I found titillation and pleasure, to be sure, but all was fleeting." He dared to glance her way and his heart clenched at how intently she listened. "Until you, Catherine. I have never had a home, not until you entered my life, and you have made my house into a sanctuary."

"But, sir, you avoid me!"

"It is not my skill to deny myself when tempted." His hand rose to her cheek again. "I want to possess you utterly, Catherine, but I fear that doing as much will mean that I lose you. I would rather have the occasional glimpse than all the physical satisfaction in the world." He swallowed. "I have made this choice to keep you by my side, but now, it turns against me, making it possible for you to abandon our match. I am sorry that I deceived you, Catherine. I entreat you to remain by my side, though I know I do not deserve it."

She stared at him, her expression unfathomable, and the moment stretched long. Rhys could not bear to hear her decision, but nor could he endure the wait for it.

There was a tap at the door and they both jumped at Forbes' appearance. The valet bowed, evidently bursting with some tidings.

"What is it, Forbes?" Rhys heard his own impatience.

"Dinner, my lord. The gong will sound in moments and I suggest your finest jacket on this night."

"Because it is Christmas Eve?"

"Because the Duke of Haynesdale has arrived, sir, out of the very teeth of the storm, and he insists that he will speak privately with you this very night."

The duke! What did he know? Why had he come?

It could be no good omen, to be sure.

Rhys' gaze rose to meet Catherine's and he knew his trepidation showed. He bent to kiss her fingertips, willing her to grant him a second chance. "My lady," he said, lifting her to her feet. "If you will excuse me."

"Of course, my lord." She nodded to the valet. "I thank you for your tidings, Forbes. I too will dress in my finest this night."

Then she was gone, retreating all too quickly to her own chamber and closing the door behind herself. Rhys closed his eyes when he heard the key turn in the lock, for he feared his wife's decision was made.

And it was not in his favor.

He should have learned that when he gambled, he invariably lost.

CHAPTER 7

Rhys said he loved her.

Catherine did not know what to make of that. The very words had made her heart flutter like a caged bird and her hands were shaking when she had retreated to her room. She wanted to believe him, but she had trusted him before—and he had tricked her.

She chose the gold dress and the crimson shawl from Rhys, and Foster set her hair in her usual style. Catherine needed her wits about her this night and if Rhys attempted to influence her thinking in his favor, he would succeed.

Could he love her? How she wished it might be true!

Why had the Duke of Haynesdale ridden through a storm to reach Rockmorton? Catherine feared she would not like whatever he had to say.

The gentleman in question met her at the bottom of the stairs. Though Catherine had known the Duke of Haynesdale for years, she had always been a little afraid of him. He was ten years her senior, a tall and imposing man of powerful physique and imposing presence. His hair was as dark as midnight with a dash of silver at the temples. His eyes were darker yet, fathomless pools glistening with intellect. He always dressed in severe black, his jackets cut from the finest cloth, his cravat as white as snow. He limped, sometimes quite badly, and he carried a substantial cane of ebony with a shining silver top, its length carved in three entwining spirals.

He was a war hero, a recluse since his return from the Peninsular Wars. His injured leg was his souvenir and there were whispers of others. She knew him, though, as a man who had come to discuss books with her father when she was a girl. She remembered him as a handsome and confident young man, one who laughed readily and was not loathe to exercise his charm. In those days, there had been no expectation of the third son of the duke ever inheriting the title, and she knew he had lived a wild life. He had been a man who filled their small sitting room when he came unexpectedly for tea, a man from another realm, and a man who admired excellent workmanship. He was said to have the most remarkable library in England, and she believed it, given his acquisitions from her father.

The man awaiting her at the bottom of the stairs she had encountered only once, at her wedding. The duke was stern now and she guessed embittered, for she felt a tide of fury emanating from him. He had lost two older brothers and his father in rapid succession, and come to the title with only a younger sister remaining. She had been wed with haste, leaving him alone at his remote manor. Her wedding had been his first appearance in society outside of the gaming hells and Catherine recalled the whispers.

"Lady Trevelaine," he said in his deep gravely voice, bowing to her politely. He drawled, just as she recalled, his words slow and deliberately uttered. She still had the old sense that he was like a predator or a hunter, one content to slowly and methodically stalk his prey.

Undoubtedly the Duke of Haynesdale was a dangerous man to his opponents even now.

His dark gaze was searching when he considered her and Catherine feared he would discern all her secrets. "I trust that you are well."

"Very well, thank you, your grace." She halted on the last step, wanting the advantage of its height. "It is an unexpected pleasure to encounter you here at Rockmorton Manor."

"I had to come," he said simply. "I received tidings that troubled me deeply."

"Surely the weather opposed your journey."

"I am not easily detained." He offered his arm and Catherine descended the last step, then took it. He led her toward the drawing room, casting her a grim glance before they reached the threshold. "I do not like when my plans go awry, my lady."

"I would not expect otherwise, your grace."

"I would speak with you in private, perhaps in the morning." He watched her closely.

"If the matter is of import, why the delay, sir?"

He flicked a glance toward the door. "No one will be leaving Rockmorton Manor soon," he growled. He turned and his gaze rose to the summit of the stairs. Rhys had stopped there, the sight of him making Catherine's heart leap. Her husband's trepidation was more than clear. "There is another discussion I would have first, before you and I consult upon your choices, my lady." The duke inclined his head to her. "If you would so indulge me."

"Of course, your grace," Catherine said because she could do nothing else. He had arranged her marriage and she understood that he saw his own word undermined or even challenged. They entered the drawing room and she was delighted to see that Eurydice had come down.

How she wished she might be present when Rhys spoke to the duke.

Either way, she had until the morning to decide whether to believe his pledge of love.

~

THE DUKE OF HAYNESDALE had changed since her last captivating sight of him, to be sure, but Esmeralda found him a thousand times more interesting than he had been as a bold and confident youth. She liked how he had become decisive, even impatient, and she did not doubt that he was stern even with himself. His gaze burned. He spoke with precision. He tolerated no fools. He was a man to control not only himself but all around him, a man possessed of a fearsome intellect and rigorous discipline, a man who could soar to the heavens with his accomplishments or reign in the lowest circles of Hell.

She watched him at dinner and wanted nothing more than to break his reserve, to seduce him so thoroughly that he roared with satisfaction—and came back to her for more.

She was of no interest to him, given her disguise, but that allowed her to watch him more openly. Indeed, Esmeralda could not tear her gaze away.

What a man.

For all the duke's grim purpose, dinner was a celebratory affair. Certainly, Montgomery's generosity was unstinted. They dined upon pheasant stuffed with a chestnut filling, with a fish course beforehand. The dining room was resplendent with greens, the crystal sparkled and the silver shone. The candles flickered, casting a golden glow over their feast, as the snow continued to fall beyond the windows. The servants were merry in anticipation of a short day on the morrow. Esmeralda guessed that there would be gifts exchanged and a fine goose for dinner. Montgomery had opened that fine bottle of port and all in the house, from guest to stableboy, was treated to a celebratory sip. The baby was brought down to be shown to all before the ladies retired, and even the duke admired the new arrival.

It was indeed a happy Christmas.

Yet Esmeralda had a definite sense that she should leave as soon as possible. She had done her best to bring the baron and his wife together, and now the duke would determine their future—unless the couple made a choice of their own. She watched the duke, so perceptive and clever, and trusted her instinct. If there was any man who could make trouble for her, it was Damien DeVries, the Duke of Haynesdale. As much as she would like to challenge him, this was not the place or the time.

Neither would she be here when he sought to blame someone if he found disfavor with the result of his intervention.

She would speak to Montgomery and leave for London at first light, if not before.

CATHERINE DID NOT HEAR Rhys return to his chamber that night. She had lingered with the ladies to await him but Montgomery had come to the library alone, noting that Rhys and the duke conferred. By the time Mrs. Oliver retired, the men had not yet emerged, so the rest of the women went to bed. Catherine had fallen asleep immediately, no doubt because of her vigil with Eurydice, and awakened early Christmas morning. She rose and dressed. In light of her pending interview with the duke, she would go down for breakfast.

She took the book, planning to return it to the library shelf before anyone could see.

She was just pushing it into place when someone spoke behind her.

"How did you know?" demanded the Duke of Haynesdale.

Catherine spun to face him as he crossed the room. If he had slept, she could not tell, for he seemed to be wearing the same jacket as the night before. Her gaze trailed to the chair turned toward the fire, which was already lit, and she wondered whether he had remained in the library all night.

"I beg your pardon, your grace?"

"How did you know that your husband had not consummated the match?"

If Catherine had been flushing before, now her cheeks burned crimson. She retrieved the book and offered it to him, her finger marking the chapter that had been so illuminating.

He looked and his dark brows rose. "Hardly a volume your father would approve for your reading."

"No, he would not." Catherine clutched her hands together before herself.

"Nor one I would expect you to seek out."

"I had to know," she said and he flicked a glance at her face. "Mrs. Oliver recommended it."

"Did she?" The duke replaced the book on the shelf, reaching the spot with ease, then retreated. "Bettencourt said that you came to him of late, initiating intimacy." He shot a glance over his shoulder. "What so provoked you?"

"There were missives left in my room, sir."

"Missives?" He sank into the chair and frowned. "Love letters?"

"No, your grace. They were said to be excerpts from a volume of conduct for ladies."

Those brows rose. "I know of no such volume that recommends a lady seduce her husband."

"It was from a manuscript. I thought perhaps the author wished to have it considered for publication." The duke's silence invited more. "It was called *The Ladies' Essential Guide to the Art of Seduction*, and most clear in its instruction of the amorous arts."

The duke's gaze sharpened. "A scandalous volume! Who was the author?"

"I do not know, sir."

He shook a finger at her. "If some individual believes that sharing such information with ladies of quality is a wise course, I will ensure that he, or she, learns the error of their ways. It is outrageous that anyone would compose such a volume for the consumption of decent women."

"I think it might be popular, your grace, though I saw only a small portion of it."

The duke glared at her, but Catherine did not cower. Then he cleared his throat and frowned, gesturing toward a sheaf of what appeared to be contracts. "You should know that Baron Trevelaine has been most accommodating."

At his gesture, Catherine stepped forward to examine them, her eyes widening as she read the first. "This is a request for an annulment of my marriage," she said, her heart sinking that Rhys had signed it.

"Yes."

The next document, though, made her heart leap with hope.

The duke continued, unaware of her reaction. "Your dowry will be returned, every shilling of it, along with the income paid to him during your marriage."

Rhys had agreed to surrender her entire legacy and dowry to her. He was granting her freedom to her, but he would pay the price. Once again, he had made a choice on principle—and she loved him for it. "But he will be left destitute."

The duke fixed her with a look. "He has lived graciously for two years longer than he deserved, at your expense. I will not tolerate that situation to continue. My obligation to your father is greater than that, and I will put right what has gone awry."

Catherine squared her shoulders. "Do you not think my opinion should have been solicited?"

"It is a matter of honor, Miss Carruthers."

Catherine almost winced to be addressed by her maiden name again.

"*My* honor," the duke continued. "I arranged the match and I will tear it asunder as the result of Bettencourt's failure to keep the agreement."

"No," Catherine said with heat. "No, your grace, you will not."

He stared at her, the air fairly crackling between them at her defiance. "I respect your commitment, even to a poor cause, but you cannot be happy," he finally said, his tone softening. "Your father will make another match for you, a more suitable one…"

"But I love Rhys Bettencourt, your grace. I will be his wife or that of no other man."

The duke rubbed his brow. "Reconsider this, Miss Carruthers. The man has signed every document without coercion to cast you from his life. You cannot imagine that he holds you in any regard or that your circumstance is destined to improve."

Catherine smiled. "But it will, sir. I will stake my all upon it. If you will excuse me, sir." With that, she clutched the documents to her chest and went in search of her lord husband.

Once on the stairs, she began to run, wanting to know the truth as soon as possible.

～

IT WAS DONE.

Rhys had not spoken to Catherine since dinner on Christmas Eve and even that had been in company. He had heard her leave her chamber early this morning and guessed what that meant. The duke had meant to speak with her early this morning, and he had spotted a carriage vanishing down the drive when he rose.

She was gone with the duke.

Rhys stood at the window of his chamber and regretted his every foolish choice. He should have courted Catherine and won her heart before this day. He should not have delayed. He should have told her the truth sooner.

And now it was too late.

The snow had stopped during the night and the sun shone brightly from a clear blue sky. Already, the snow was melting and the paths had been cleared. The snow appeared to be less deep in the garden but still it twinkled in the morning light, like a field of diamonds.

All the same, Rhys felt irritable and impatient, both wanting to be home and dreading his arrival at that house when it was devoid of Catherine's presence. It would have to be sold, of course. Everything would have to be sold, and he did not care.

How ironic that he had been prepared to wed anyone two years before to keep his holdings, and now he was indifferent to its fate. Without Catherine, the future yawned before him, an eternity of emptiness.

Rhys shoved a hand through his hair, debating the merit of summoning Forbes when he heard a key turn. He spun to see the door to the adjacent chamber opening. Against every expectation, Catherine appeared in the portal.

She even smiled at him.

She was wearing her blue dress, the one she often chose for travel, and carried a familiar sheaf of papers.

Rhys stared, unable to understand why she was not in the carriage that was already headed for London. "You are still here."

"I am." She smiled. "Dare I hope that you are not disappointed?"

He shook his head, finding himself without words.

Catherine put down the papers on the chair by the fire. She smiled and reached to run her fingertips along his chin. Rhys thought his heart would explode and he stood utterly still, fearful of making any move that might dissuade her. "I had to explain your error to you. It seemed only right."

"Error?"

"You are not reasonable, Rhys."

"Do you chide me apurpose?" he asked and she laughed a little.

"I would correct your error, no more and no less." She met his gaze steadily and the sight of her resolve made him want to defend her from every threat, even himself. "Life is full of risk. We are at risk at every moment."

"But..."

She stretched to brush her lips across his mouth, silencing him with a touch that set him simmering, her eyes vehemently blue. "How many horses have you ridden, though many people have been thrown from the saddle and injured or even killed?" she asked, her words soft but heated. "How many carriages have you taken, even though many have been injured in accidents involving those vehicles? How many fires have been lit on your hearth, despite the fact that many houses burn to the ground, taking all within to their graves?"

"I..."

"How many meals have you eaten, uncertain of the cleanliness of the kitchen or the intentions of those preparing the food, all the while aware that you might be poisoned or made ill? How many ships have you boarded, knowing there is always a prospect of drowning on rough waters?" She shook her head. "Life abounds with risk, Rhys, and to avoid it all is to surrender the pleasure of living."

"But surely some risks should be shunned."

"Not all of them," she argued, hesitated. "Not this one, Rhys," she added, then kissed him. Her kiss was tentative, light and sweet, and utterly persuasive. Rhys felt his objections melting, as the snow did before the sun. She leaned her forehead on his chest, the scent of her hair rising to tempt him, the fan of her breath against his skin pure torment. "I saw what Eurydice endured, and saw her smile at the precious result of her labor. That child is glorious and he will be cherished—and she has no regret for her own suffering. It was worth it, Rhys," she insisted, giving his robe a shake. "And I would accept this same risk to conceive your child."

"You should not…"

"But I will." She smiled at him, her gaze bright. "You taught me that, Rhys, to take a risk to defend what I believe to be important." If his throat was not tight enough, it became more so with her next words. "I can do nothing else, since I love you with all my heart."

"Catherine!" Despite the marvel of this confession, he had to make her understand. "But the duke vows he will arrange a better match for you."

"I have no desire for one. My current match satisfies me in every way." She turned away from him then and he wished he could see her eyes. She picked up the first of the infernal documents and seemed to be reading it.

"Our match will be annulled, Catherine."

She held the document by a corner and cast a coquettish glance over her shoulder at him, one that made his heart skip. "It can only be annulled if we are too closely related, which we are not, or if it is unconsummated." To his astonishment, she lowered the document into the fire, smiling as the parchment lit. "I think, sir, that we might remedy any shortfall in that situation."

Rhys could only stare as hope flooded his heart.

"A son would secure your legacy and the presence of children, boys or girls, would fill our home with joy. Your child, Rhys, would make our marriage complete."

"Our child," he corrected, his voice thick. His hand rose to tangle in her hair, so in awe was he of his wife in this moment.

She smiled a little and flushed, his statue melting into the goddess who owned his heart. "Our child," she agreed then smiled. "I suggest we begin the quest immediately, for I have learned that today is most appropriate for the conception of a child." Her smile turned so wicked that he could only stare. "And Mrs. Grieves would take pleasure in it, to be sure."

"Never mind Mrs. Grieves!" Rhys said with a laugh and she laughed along with him. He caught her close and kissed her sweetly, cherishing her even more in this moment. "You are certain."

"I am committed to this new cause," she said, then lowered her gaze. "I am advised that there is pleasure that makes the risk worth taking." Her words were so softly uttered that he could barely hear them. She looked up then, impaling him with a glance. "Introduce me to this pleasure, Rhys, that we might both embrace this risk without regret. Let us be wed in every way from this day forward."

She was so forthright, so strong, so sensible—and yet so completely alluring. Rhys could not have denied her anything in that moment, not even for his own life.

"I will, my Catherine," he vowed, framing her face in his hands. "I will. But remember that you must ensure that I am right in the details. I have no knowledge of successful marriage."

"How fortunate that I do." she said with a smile.

"Perfect partners," he said. "Each complementing the other."

She tilted her head to study him, her eyes dancing. "Perhaps even a match that was destined to be."

"There is no perhaps about it, my Catherine." They stared at each other in wonder for a long moment, and Rhys knew his heart was not the only one full to bursting. Then he kissed his wife as he had never kissed her before, pouring his all into the embrace.

She was the home he had never known he desired, the key to making his world complete. He would spend the rest of his life ensuring her happiness and striving to be a man worthy of her affections. He would do whatever he could to prompt her smile, even break his deathbed promise to his father.

It was time to prove the depth of his affection to her, and Rhys knew he would never tire of that joyous task.

~

GOODNESS.

Catherine clung to Rhys as the morning sunlight shone through the window. As ever, the sunbeams tangled in his hair, burnishing the auburn waves to gold, but on this day, she ran her fingers through those curls with possessive ease. She had never imagined that two people could find such pleasure together and she knew her satisfaction showed in her smile when Rhys lifted his head. He kissed her again, slowly and sweetly, and her heart raced with delight as she returned his embrace.

It was when he was slumbering beside her that she

realized there was something white upon the carpet at the door. Catherine knew immediately what it had to be. She eased out of bed without disturbing Rhys and retrieved the note, putting on her glasses to read it.

Upon the merit of variety.

In intimate matters, as in all other pursuits, variety ensures that the endeavor does not become routine or dull. Invitation, surprise, audacity and interruption all play their part in securing a gentleman's ongoing attention, but so do attentiveness, playfulness and a measure of innovation. While each couple invariably finds a formula that reliably provides satisfaction, be sure to welcome a measure of novelty in the bedroom. A spirit of discovery will go a long way to keep a spark alight—and warrant many, many years of mutual pleasure.

Catherine smiled and folded the note, watching Rhys sleep as she tucked it into her pocket. Foster tapped lightly then, appearing with Catherine's breakfast tray. Her eyes rounded at the sight of Rhys asleep in Catherine's bed, though Catherine held a finger to her lips for silence.

"Oh, my lady," the maid whispered with undisguised delight.

"Perhaps my husband would welcome a tray this morning."

"I wager he would, my lady!" And Foster was gone, the sound of her running feet audible on the carpeted corridor. Catherine returned to the bed and sat beside Rhys, running her fingertips over his shoulder. He stirred and smiled up at her with lazy satisfaction.

"Happy Christmas, Rhys."

"Happy Christmas, Catherine." His smile turned wicked as she bent to kiss him. "Lock the door, temptress. I believe we will be late today."

And that suggestion suited Catherine very well indeed.

~

SINCE THERE WAS no prospect of making their way to church that Christmas morning, the entire household were summoned to the library at Montgomery's instruction. Rhys found his step light for he was buoyed with a sense of well-being. The house smelled of roast goose and there was a festive sense of anticipation in the air. It did not hurt that Catherine held his arm, her face flushed with delight and her eyes sparkling. He placed his hand over hers as they stood near the fire together. The Duke of Haynesdale considered them for a long moment before he sat down.

"Your aunt declines to join us," the duke noted when all were assembled and Montgomery raised a hand for silence.

"Aunt Delilah has returned to London this morning," their host said and the duke's disapproval was clear. "She said her gout made her a poor guest and sends her best wishes for the day to all." There was a murmur of approval at this, but the duke scowled.

"How well do you know this aunt of yours, Montgomery?" he demanded.

Montgomery blinked. "Not at all. I was unaware of her existence until she wrote to me in December." He smiled. "But family must gather together for the Yule."

The duke's brow darkened. "I fear that woman may not have been your aunt, but an imposter," he said.

Montgomery gave a gasp of surprise that seemed a little vehement to Rhys.

The countess developed a keen interest in her son, a hint that she knew more of this matter.

Rhys was intrigued. He exchanged a glance with Catherine but she shrugged.

"I will uncover the truth," the duke vowed softly.

Meanwhile, Montgomery made a charming speech about the weather and his newly arrived son, prompting merry laughter from all. Then he opened the Bible and read of the Nativity, to the satisfaction of all.

There was punch, brought from the kitchen, and they toasted each other and the season, before the servants returned to their duties and Montgomery led his wife and guests to the dining room.

As they celebrated a happy Christmas together, Rhys could not help wondering whether the duke was right.

London—several days later

As much as Esmeralda had enjoyed the ruse and her Christmas at Rockmorton Manor, it was a relief to return to London and shed her disguise.

She and Ophelia returned to London in Montgomery's carriage, then had left his house in a cab. It had been a frantic journey, made with all the haste they could manage. They had changed cabs twice after leaving Montgomery's London house, ultimately ending up at the closed theatre. There, they retreated to a dressing room.

Esmeralda could not deny that the possibility of the Duke of Haynesdale in pursuit gave her a welcome thrill. It might be worth having him uncover the truth.

The myriad veils and horrific coat were the first to go, then the wig that itched beyond all else.

"Keep it all," Esmeralda advised the actress. "I may have need of the costume again."

Ophelia laughed. "After such a success, I should expect a curtain call." The actress had taken to her role as a lady's maid with more enthusiasm than Esmeralda might have expected. And her performance as Perkins had been brilliant, utterly plausible and perfect.

For the first time since embarking on the adventure, the two could speak openly about the feint. Their gazes met in the mirror and they both smiled.

"A triumph," Ophelia said with admiration. "You were perfection."

"I did enjoy it," Esmeralda admitted. "How liberating it was to say whatsoever one desired, however rude it might be! How delicious to be forthright—and humored because of my supposed age. There are definite benefits to growing older that I had not considered before."

"Beyond that, look at the change in the baroness!" Ophelia enthused. "When they arrived, she was a sad little mouse, but she was glorious by Christmas."

"Absolutely radiant."

"Indeed. They owe their happiness to you, Esmeralda."

Success was a potent brew, to be sure. Esmeralda winced as the mask was finally pulled from her skin, then rubbed her nose vigorously. "It has been itching in the worst way."

"These masks always do," Ophelia said, returning it carefully to a box. She had used her skills from the theatre to construct a mask of thin cloth soaked in glue, shaping it to Esmeralda's face, then adding myriad wrinkles and features more pronounced than Esmeralda's own. It covered Esmeralda from hairline to bosom, the edges concealed by an elaborate wig and her clothes and stoles. Layers of glue and paint had been added, then it had been made up, just as woman's face might be. Esmeralda had also worn padding beneath her corset to thicken her waist and more padding in her gloves to make her fingers appear thick and gnarled.

The costume was uncomfortable and warm, but no one would ever recognize her. "It's the glue in the cloth. Be glad you don't have to wear it on stage, for the footlights add to the heat."

"I never realized how you suffered for your art." Esmeralda fastidiously cleaned the bits of gum from her face. Truth be told, it was a relief to look in the mirror and see her own self, not the hideous visage of Mrs. Oliver. And her waist seemed to be gloriously slender after these past weeks. She felt a new appreciation of her charms. "I could never have done this without you, Ophelia."

"I enjoyed it mightily. Thank you for inviting me to participate."

"And you have all of the pages?"

"Save that last one. I retrieved them each time she left her room. No one suspected a thing." Ophelia surrendered a sheaf of papers and Esmeralda fanned through them, ensuring that the other pages were present.

The one she had left on Christmas morning had been fairly innocuous, though she wished it had been possible to retrieve it, too.

"There must be no evidence of my involvement," she said and the actress nodded.

"But the tale will spread, rely upon it. Mrs. Oliver may be in great demand."

Esmeralda laughed. "Then it is good that I could write volumes on the seduction of men."

"You may have to," Ophelia noted. "By the way, may I borrow those notes now that our charade is done? One must always seize the opportunity to learn from a mistress of her craft."

"Of course." Esmeralda donned her usual clothing and surveyed herself with greater satisfaction than she had thought possible. Her heart was light and her enthusiasm for the season ahead was high. Would others seek the counsel of *The Ladies' Essential Guide to the Art of Seduction?* Would she encounter the Duke of Haynesdale in town this season?

Esmeralda could not wait to find out.

~

UPON A MIDNIGHT CLEAR

BONUS EPILOGUE FOR THE CHRISTMAS CONQUEST

CHAPTER 1

London—April 16, 1817

Rhys Bettencourt, Baron Trevelaine, and his wife, Catherine, were returning home after a pleasurable evening at the theatre. The day had been unseasonably warm and the fog was thick as a result, which meant they made slow but steady progress. The fog swirled beyond the windows in a wall of white, as if they drove through clouds, and Rhys could only guess their location. The sounds of the horses' hooves seemed overly loud; the light from the lamps on the coach did not penetrate the fog, and they might have been alone in this city of millions. In truth, he did not mind, so long as Catherine was by his side.

They had seen a production of Shakespeare's *Macbeth* and he could not keep himself from expecting at least one of the witches to step out of the fog to challenge them.

The notion made him frown.

"You are pensive," Catherine said lightly, pressing his hand. "I suppose you are thinking of curses and destiny." Her tone revealed her own pragmatic view of such superstitions.

He turned to her with a smile. She wore her fair hair more loosely since Christmas and he thought the change suited her well. Overall, she chose more vivid colors and spoke with greater confidence, as if the newfound intimacy between them had made her blossom from a bud to a glorious rose. On this night, her dress was a deep sapphire that made her eyes seem more deeply blue and her skin more perfectly fair. Her smile never failed to make his heart thunder and he guessed the direction of her thoughts in this moment. He was not entirely dissuaded of the power of his family curse but tried to forget it for the sake of her happiness.

"On the contrary, I was thinking of Mrs. Oliver," he admitted.

Catherine's brows rose. "Why?"

"When I first met her, I was reminded of the witches in the Scottish play."

"That is curious." His wife's gaze had slid to the opposite window and Rhys had a fleeting impression that she knew something he did not. But there were no longer any secrets between them. "What a night this is," she said, as if to change the subject, and he wondered.

"What do you know of Mrs. Oliver that I do not?"

Catherine laughed. "Nothing that would give you pleasure."

"Now I *am* intrigued."

"And you must remain so," she said, touching her fingertip to his lips. "For I am sworn to secrecy."

"Even from me?"

"Especially from you."

Rhys frowned and might have asked, but Catherine kissed him sweetly.

"Trust me," she whispered and he sighed in concession, because he did.

"Only if you will confide in me when you can."

"I swear it to you, Rhys."

It was not entirely satisfactory, but he would accept her terms.

"Why did she remind you of the witches?" Catherine asked.

Rhys shrugged. "There was something about her appearance that did not seem right, though I cannot name it precisely." His wife did not reply. "Do you think the duke was right, that she was an imposter and not Montgomery's aunt at all?"

"It seems possible."

That had to be it. "What if her appearance was contrived, with a disguise like that worn by an actor?" Catherine straightened slightly and Rhys knew he was right. "What if we knew her but did not recognize her?"

"What a remarkable notion."

"Would you not want to unveil her, if hers was a deception?"

"No, I would not." Catherine spoke so crisply that he was startled. She turned to him, her expression intent. "I know only a little more of her than you, but have pledged not to speak of it further. And the truth is, Rhys, that I promised as much willingly. I owe that lady my infinite gratitude, for it is due to Mrs. Oliver, that our match has become so amiable."

"She left the notes in your chamber," he guessed.

Catherine nodded, ceding that much. "Without their counsel, I would have left your home for that of my father, and neither of us would have been glad of that."

"How did you confirm that she left those notes?"

Catherine's smile was mischievous. "I will not break my pledge for you, sir, no matter how you charm me."

Rhys laughed and pulled her closer for a kiss.

"But in truth, I could not imagine who else might have done so," she continued when she could. "The servants would not have dared. Eurydice confessed immediately that she did not write them and I doubt that Montgomery would feel any inclination to grant me such advice." She nodded once. "Reason led me to Mrs. Oliver, notwithstanding the fact that she gave me the book."

Rhys winced at the mention of the book that had revealed his deception. That had been a moment of much consternation, though all had ended well. "But why would she stir herself to try to influence our marriage?"

"Perhaps you *do* know her," Catherine said mysteriously. "Perhaps she cares for you and wishes to see you happy."

"I cannot imagine who would be so concerned."

"And I do not care," Catherine said, giving him a kiss that silenced any further comment he might have made. "It is the result that is of import, no more and no less," she added softly, then kissed him again.

Rhys growled and pulled her into his lap, capturing her mouth beneath his own and kissing her soundly until she sighed with delight. She set aside his hat, then pushed her fingers into his hair, drawing him close and kissing him with an ardor that still shook him to his marrow. He slid a hand beneath her skirts and she arched against him, welcoming his caress so that his heart pounded.

"I thought you meant to warn me of curses," she whispered in his ear, grazing his ear lobe with her teeth. The fan of her breath against his skin, the scent of her perfume, the press of her breasts against his chest all conspired to make it impossible to think of more than pleasing and possessing her. "Since this is a most auspicious night and one we should not ignore."

Rhys pulled back to look into her eyes, his heart in his throat. "Tonight?"

"Tonight," Catherine confirmed without hesitation. She held his gaze. "By the calculations taught to me by Mrs. Oliver."

Rhys felt his old fear surge and he held her more tightly against him, wanting to remain in this moment forever.

Catherine's gloved fingertip slid across his lips and she reached to whisper in his ear. "I love that you fear for me," she whispered and he closed his eyes. "I am honored that you love me, Rhys, for I love you as well. But do not mistake misfortune for an unshakable curse. My mother delivered safely of three children and I will deliver at least as many to you." He met her gaze, knowing she saw the secrets of his heart. She smiled and brushed her lips across his. "Let us make an heir tonight. Trust me, Rhys."

Rhys took a breath and nodded. "I do."

Her smile turned wicked. "Then I beg of you, love me, sir, all the night long."

Rhys could only smile in return. "I will," he vowed and would have kissed her again, but the coach halted as Fielding shouted to the horses. They were before Trevelaine House and the moment to surrender to Catherine's invitation had arrived.

He would make this a night to remember.

CATHERINE KNEW that Rhys still had concerns for her welfare. It was only natural, given the number of women in his family who had died in childbirth, but Catherine had no intention of joining their number. The sole way to prove as much to Rhys was to deliver of a healthy son, and survive the feat of doing as much.

Though, truly, it was not that goal alone that had her joining him abed most nights. She had learned so much of pleasure from Rhys, so much of satisfaction that it was hard to believe that a mere four months before, she had possessed no notion of the possibilities. The excerpts had launched her on a path of discovery and it seemed each night brought new revelations. Now she knew Rhys' body as well as her own. She knew what excited him and what pleased him. She could time the very instant when a caress would drive him wild and knew precisely how to touch him to increase his pleasure. Similarly, he had learned her own preferences and introduced her to sensations that she could not imagine abandoning. Their chambers had become havens of pleasure and satisfaction, likely to be explored at all hours of the day and night. They always slept together, in one bed or the other, and both Foster and Forbes had ceased to be surprised by wherever they encountered the couple in the morning.

Even better, they labored together as a team in improving his estates. They set upon a problem each month and each gathered information and resources to see it resolved, conferred, budgeted, planned and succeeded. The cottages for the tenants had been improved near Trevelaine Manor and a doctor had been convinced to take up his residence and practice in Trevelaine Hollow nearby. Rhys was embarking upon a new system of crop rotation in the fields, and his tenants were both avid supporters and participants. He himself spent an afternoon per month in the public house in Trevelaine Hollow, where all knew he could be approached, which invited confidences that tenants did not wish to bring to the hall. His properties prospered beneath his attentive eye and Catherine was glad to be a part of their development.

Similarly, he had introduced her to the pleasures of

the theater. They had attended balls and dances this winter and she grew more confident in social exchanges than she had been before. It was wondrous to have his encouragement and approval, and she yearned to provide the one additional thing that would secure his happiness.

An heir.

On this night, Catherine was thinking of the merit of surprise and bold choices. There had been another addition to the growing compilation of advice from Mrs. Oliver, a very specific means of surprising a gentleman that Catherine was prepared to try.

THE HOUSE WAS quiet by the time they arrived, most of the servants having retired at the late hour. Henderson, the butler, opened the door for them, attired as impeccably as ever—Catherine had long ago decided that the older man never slept. He was always inscrutable and proper, though she sensed that perhaps he had warmed slightly to her presence in his master's house.

Foster awaited Catherine in her chamber, the young maid's eyes alight with curiosity. She peppered Catherine with questions about the play, most notably about who was in the audience. Catherine could not answer them all for she had been aware only of Rhys, sitting beside her and holding her hand, casting her the occasional smile. His thigh had been so close to her own that she had felt the warmth emanating from his body and she had been tempted to caress him in the shadows. Time and even familiarity had not diminished his effect upon her.

The blue silk robe had been left behind at Rockmorton Manor, with regret, but it had been replaced by two similar garments, one in crimson silk embroidered with gold and one of that deep sapphire blue Catherine favored. Her hair brushed out to a sheen and hanging to her waist, she chose the red one and dismissed Foster. Barefoot with the robe hanging open, she took a candle and knocked upon the door to her husband's chamber.

Rhys himself opened it, his slow smile of welcome heating her as surely as his touch. Catherine was vaguely aware that a door closed behind his valet, Forbes, but she was lost in the glittering green of Rhys' eyes. He, too, wore a robe, this one of green silk, and she could see his chest where it hung open. His chamber was in darkness, just like her own, and the light from the candle gilded him, burnishing the handsome lines of his face, glinting in his auburn hair, illuminating him against the shadows.

"Good evening, my lady," he murmured in a seductively low voice. "Is something amiss?"

"Indeed, sir," she replied as she knew he expected. "I find myself in desperate need of a satisfaction only you can deliver." His smile was all the encouragement she needed. Catherine swept his robe open with a fingertip, placed her hand over his thundering heart, and bent to kiss his other nipple. She felt his heart skip and heard him catch his breath, then flicked her tongue against the nipple to coax it to a peak.

Rhys gasped and tipped back his head, surrendering to her scheme, whatever it might be.

She took her time about the endeavor, knowing Rhys liked it slow, and smiled a little when she felt his hand slide into her hair. His fingers were warm and strong, his touch possessive, and she loved it. She used her tongue and her teeth until his nipple was a taut bead, then turned her attention to its mate. She let her hand slide down the smooth strength of his stomach. He inhaled sharply when she closed her hand around him and his grip tightened in her hair as he raised her face to his.

"Temptress," he whispered, his eyes glowing with desire. "How fortunate that I find myself experiencing the same desperate need."

She pretended to pout. "That only you can satisfy?"

Rhys laughed heartily, until she caressed him boldly and silenced his laughter. He was taut then, his eyes glittering, but he waited for her move. "Only you, Catherine," he confessed, his voice hoarse. "Only you will suffice." With that, he took the candle and snuffed it, his gaze locked with hers. He then claimed her other hand, leading her to his bed. There was only the light from the fire on the hearth to illuminate the chamber with its golden glow. Catherine dropped her robe, well aware of her husband's gaze fixed upon her and climbed onto the bed, kneeling on the mattress to face him. He cast his own robe aside and came to her, his interest more than clear.

"I thought to be bold this night," she admitted and watched his eyes flash.

"I am your servant, my lady," he growled before claiming her lips in a possessive kiss. His caress was a little rough, thrilling in its demand, and Catherine responded in kind. She caught his face in her hands and kissed him hungrily, feasting upon his mouth, feeling the heat rise to a crescendo between them. She ran her hands over him and when he locked his hands around her waist, she arched against him, rubbing her breasts against his chest, loving how readily she could feed his desire. She wound her arms around his neck, opening her mouth to him, then gave him a little tug.

Rhys tumbled to the bed, then rolled onto the mattress with her cradled against his chest. He kissed her nipple when she was atop him, one hand sliding between her thighs to caress her intimately as he held her captive with his other arm around her waist. She felt his jolt of surprise when he discovered how aroused she was and she laughed a little, urging him to his back

"You are my servant this night, by your own admission," she protested and he smiled.

He raised his hands as he stared up at her, admiration in his eyes. "Then I must pay you homage," he whispered huskily. Before Catherine could object, she found herself on her back with Rhys looming over her.

His gaze was filled with intent and he watched her as he slid his hands down the length of her, a leisurely caress that launched a fire beneath her skin. He held her gaze as he kissed her nipple, drawing it to a point as he teased it with his tongue and his teeth. He tormented her until she squirmed with pleasure, watching her all the while, then turned his attention upon her other breast. His hand closed over the first, and he rolled that tight nipple between his finger and thumb. An eternity later, he eased lower, raining kisses over her stomach, his hands sliding down to her thighs. Catherine caught her breath in anticipation and parted her legs, gasping as he kissed her in that most intimate of places.

This kiss was a glorious pleasure, one that overwhelmed her every time. She closed her eyes and arched her back, surrendering to the satisfaction Rhys was determined to give. The tumult rose within her as he continued his sensory assault, then all too soon, she cried out in her release.

As ever, when she caught her breath and opened her eyes, she found Rhys looming over her, his expression filled with satisfaction as he wiped his mouth.

"You like to torment me," she whispered and he grinned.

"I like to see your release." His eyes glittered. "There is nothing like it, Catherine. You are my fiery goddess come to life." He arched a brow. "Or maybe to smite me. I would not complain of either fate."

Catherine laughed and reached for him, kissing him as she rolled him to his back. She ran her hands over the hard planes of Rhys' body, boldly caressing him. She ran the flat of her palm down the length of him from shoulder to knee, pausing to caress him with sure strokes that made him inhale sharply. When he was larger and harder than she'd ever seen him, she straddled him, watching his eyes widen with surprise. She held his gaze as she placed him inside her, watching his consternation and admiring his control. Then she slowly lowered herself, taking his strength inside her in slow increments.

Rhys gasped. His eyes darkened. His jaw tensed. She saw his pulse at his throat and savored her power over this remarkable man, her defender and protector, her husband and her champion. She moved slowly and deliberately, mustering the storm within him, watching his every reaction to prolong his pleasure.

It seemed an eternity until she had him sheathed within her, a most satisfactory situation.

"Merciless," he whispered, clearly enjoying his situation.

Catherine rolled her hips, watching him swallow, and smiled. "And I have only just begun," she murmured. It took another eternity for her to rise up on her knees, then slowly claim him again. Rhys groaned when she moved to do as much a third time and she couldn't resist him. When he was inside her again, she lowered herself over him, caught his face in her hands and kissed him with newfound demand. Rhys met her touch for touch, one arm locked around her waist, his tongue dueling with hers and his passion hot enough to scorch.

Then his other hand eased between them, caressing

her with a surety that set her blood afire. Catherine was the one who moaned now and she rode him faster and harder, encouraged by his touch. Sparks had to be flying from her fingers as the familiar tumult grew inside her, as she gripped his shoulders and rocked atop him with greater and greater fervor. His touch was demanding and relentless, driving her toward her satisfaction with a persistence that could not be denied.

Suddenly, the heat rose to a crescendo, Rhys pinched her with surety and Catherine cried out as she was suffused with pleasure. A heartbeat later, Rhys rolled her to her back and drove deep inside her, roaring as he found his own satisfaction.

They lay together, limbs entangled, catching their breath as the fire crackled on the hearth. Rhys braced himself on an elbow and smiled down at her, drawing her hair from her face with a gentle fingertip. "May I guess that you have been inspired?"

Catherine laughed. "I cannot speak of it, sir."

"Ah, secrets. I confess I have no quibbles with the impact of this one." He kissed her soundly, showing his satisfaction. His eyes gleamed when he lifted his head. "Allow me, my lady, to be of service to you at any time."

Catherine smiled. She had never expected such joy in marriage, but she had found it with Rhys—and she would savor every moment they had together. "I believe I will require your services again before the dawn, sir."

"As you wish," Rhys murmured. "Perhaps twice would be better," he added wickedly and her heart warmed that he, too, was committed to her plan.

Then he kissed her soundly and there was only the pleasures of their union to be savored.

CHAPTER 2

December 23, 1817 – London

f Catherine Bettencourt had her way, this would be the most perfect of Christmases. Trevelaine House was filled with greens, the larder was overflowing with delicious provisions, and their guests would begin to arrive in the morning. She had invited Rhys' two nephews and their fathers to celebrate the season with them, and both Mr. Bessborough and Mr. Pierpont had accepted with undisguised delight. Eurydice and Montgomery were in Cornwall, but had sent their best regards.

Catherine's father and her younger sisters, Patricia and Prudence, would come for both Christmas Eve and Christmas Day, though they would not be staying as houseguests. Carruthers House was not that distant, though it was not in as fashionable a neighborhood as Trevelaine House. Even the Duke of Haynesdale had ceded that he might join them briefly on Christmas Day before honoring his other engagements.

It was late in the afternoon of a sunny, cold day and

159

Catherine was in the library, reviewing her lists, ensuring that she had not overlooked a single detail. Rhys had left earlier, his mysterious manner indicating that his destination was a shop and his objective a present for herself. Catherine had already bought him a snuff-box, set with his initials, and embroidered a handkerchief with the same.

She reviewed the menus yet again, counting the side dishes and the pickles, amending her list of necessary dishes and serving pieces. They would have fish on Christmas Eve, followed by roast beef, then two geese would be roasted on Christmas Day, given the number of their guests. There would also be cold ham, in case there was need of more. Did they even possess silver asparagus tongs? She would have to ask Henderson. The puddings had been baked and the shortbread, too, with additional sweets having been acquired from Brisbane's Emporium. The house had smelled wonderful in recent days. There were additional stores of wine and brandy in the cellar, the silver had been polished and the linens pressed to perfection. The chambers for their guests had been prepared and she hoped that every amenity had been provided. She checked her lists again.

Though she did not share Rhys' superstition about childbirth, the rounding of her belly certainly made her consider the statistical possibilities.

If she did not survive the arrival of the child, likely to be in late January, she wanted to give Rhys this perfect Christmas celebration—and ensure that his family connections were forged even stronger than they had become.

"Tea, my lady?" Henderson enquired from the doorway.

"I didn't ring," Catherine said with surprise.

The older man, remarkably, smiled. "But you have

been busy all the day long, my lady. It seemed that you might be desirous of a little refreshment."

"It is a welcome notion, Henderson. I thank you." When the butler might have left, Catherine asked. "Do we possess silver asparagus tongs?"

"Two pair, my lady, and they have been polished for Christmas Day. I believe that is when you plan to have the asparagus served."

"Yes, with the bechamel sauce."

"Of course." His silver brows rose and he added in a gentler tone. "I believe that all is well in hand for the festive season, my lady."

Catherine smiled and put aside her lists. "You are right, of course, Henderson. I simply wish for everything to be perfect."

"I am certain that the baron would insist matters already are."

"Perhaps I am more demanding than my husband."

The butler's eyes twinkled. "I daresay you are, my lady, and it is a most welcome change. This house has had need of a firm hand for many years and it prospers beneath yours."

Catherine realized she had been complimented, and by the most unlikely of people. She felt herself flush. "I thank you, Henderson. That is high praise from you. I confess I found Trevelaine House a little daunting three years ago."

"One would never imagine as much, my lady. It is as if you were born to such responsibilities."

The pair eyed each other with newfound and mutual respect. "Tea would be lovely, Henderson. Perhaps in the drawing room?"

The older man bowed. "As you wish, my lady."

Catherine rose from her seat, still amazed that it took her a moment to gain her balance each time she stood up. Would she ever see her toes again? They had indeed conceived a son that April night after the theater, and her belly had rounded with remarkable speed. The doctor pronounced himself satisfied that all would be well, and after those first few queasy months, she felt quite well. Rhys fussed over her, of course.

Next time, he would likely fuss just as much. The man was protective to a fault.

Catherine moved around the desk carefully, only to halt and seize the edge of it at a stab of pain.

She stood and blinked in awe as the contraction rippled through her. It faded finally, giving her time to marvel at the sensation, then her water broke with gusto. She gasped at yet another new sensation and gripped the desk.

"Henderson!" she managed to call. "I will have need of the midwife, if you please."

The butler appeared in the doorway immediately, his eyes widening at the sight before him. "I beg you to sit down, my lady," he said brusquely, bringing her a straight chair.

Catherine sank down upon it with gratitude, catching her breath as a second contraction began to build. Already? Surely it should not come so soon?

But there was no one to ask, for Henderson had left her, and the book she had borrowed from Eurydice was in her bedchamber, far away. She heard Henderson shouting for Foster and dispatching a footman to the midwife, his urgency audible. She tried to school her fear, which raged now that the moment was upon her.

In this moment, all she wanted was Rhys.

～

THE PARURE WAS PRECISELY as Rhys had ordered. "Truly, you have outdone yourself," he said to the jeweller, who smiled with pride. "The sapphires are perfectly matched. Each is as deeply blue as the next and the gradation of sizes across the necklace is most attractive." The sapphires had been cut into faceted teardrops, with the largest hanging at the middle of the necklace. There were seven of them on the necklace, set with gold filigree in between, and two of the middle size hung from the earrings. The coordinating headpiece was all filigree with a single oval blue stone in the middle. The bracelet and ring, similarly, were each graced with a single sapphire surrounded by the golden swirls. The setting made the most of the stones, in Rhys' view, and he knew that Catherine would look like a queen when she wore it.

"I am glad you are pleased, sir."

"It will suit my wife very well," Rhys said, watching as it was carefully packaged for him. The cases were of deep blue velvet lined with white satin, each piece having its place.

"A special occasion, sir?"

"Many occasions, to be sure. It is Christmas, our third anniversary and the lady will soon deliver of our first child."

"An abundance of blessings, then," the jeweller concluded with a smile. "And well worthy of such a celebration." He bowed his head and presented the package. "I thank you for your custom, my lord."

"And I thank you for your skill," Rhys replied, then tucked the parcel under his arm. He debated the merit of stopping at Brisbane's to add a length of coordinating silk to his gift that Catherine might have a new dress, too, but he went to the dressmaker with her. They could choose the cloth together. A new dress after the baby was born would be most welcome. He knew she found her current dimensions a little distressing, as natural as they were.

In truth, he was intent upon returning home with

haste, though he could not have said why. Usually, he liked to linger on Regent Street in this season, when everyone seemed to be filled with goodwill, but he would have preferred to do as much with Catherine. He smiled in anticipation as he rode through the busy streets, certain that the festivities she had planned would make for a fine Christmas indeed.

He was not prepared for Henderson to lunge out of the house at the appearance of the carriage, much less for his usually impassive butler to appear alarmed. "My lord! The child comes!"

"Not yet!" Rhys protested. "The doctor said the end of January."

"The child did not heed his counsel," Henderson replied grimly.

It was true. The time had come.

Rhys gave instructions for the parcel to be put in the safe, then took the stairs three at a time. The midwife tried to keep him from his wife's chamber, but she failed utterly in that endeavor.

"Catherine?"

She was in her bed, pale with wide eyes. Of course, she was wearing her glasses and clutched the book she had borrowed from the countess of Rockmorton.

"Rhys, it proceeds very quickly," she said, and he heard the fear in her voice. When she grimaced at a contraction, Rhys ignored the midwife's instruction that he should leave. He shed his jacket and took his place beside his wife.

"Sir!" the midwife said. "This is not customary…"

"This situation is my responsibility," he said, holding fast to Catherine's shoulders. She gripped his hand and he knew she was glad of his presence. "Tell me what I can do."

~

WHAT FOLLOWED WERE the longest eight hours of Rhys' life. He found himself both terrified and awed by the force of nature that he witnessed that day. He was also impressed by Catherine's fortitude and her resolve. Whatever the midwife instructed her to do, she did. However fierce each contraction, she mustered her strength for the next. In between, when possible, she consulted the details described in the book.

He held her hand and rubbed her back, he urged her onward when she faltered and he wiped her tears. She squeezed his hand during her contractions and he did not care if she wrenched it from his arm. The charm sent by Eurydice was nearly shredded from her squeezing of it, though Rhys supposed that was its purpose. She was panting when the midwife said the babe's head was appearing. Catherine gritted her teeth and pushed as instructed, her hair damp with perspiration, and Rhys was amazed yet again by his wife.

When the babe gave its first cry, his relief was so profound that he shook with it.

"A boy," the midwife said with triumph and he watched as she tied and cut the cord.

A boy.

Then he realized that Catherine was smiling up at him.

"You were hoping for a girl, sir," she teased, her eyes sparkling, and Rhys knew he should not have been surprised that she had guessed his secret. He bent and kissed her sweetly, then turned to the midwife, who had surrendered the infant to her apprentice to be washed.

"And the lady?" he asked, barely daring to voice the words.

The midwife smiled. "A robust lady, to be sure," she said, giving Catherine's knee a familiar pat. "And one in a hurry to see the matter resolved."

"A hurry?" Catherine echoed then laughed a little. "It took forever."

"The first is either quick or takes an eon," the midwife said. "Oh, there is the rest of it." She bent over Catherine then winked when she straightened, to Rhys' surprise. "I expect this will be the first of many children, my lord. When it is so easily done, there is no reason to be shy about it."

"Another son," Catherine said with conviction, committing to a repeat of this endeavor before Rhys had acknowledged his relief at this one's successful conclusion.

"An heir and a spare," the midwife agreed cheerfully.

He looked between them with astonishment.

Catherine smiled. "And I should love at least one girl," she said wistfully.

Three? They would have two more children? Rhys sat down hard on the closest chair, watching his Catherine laugh at him.

"Rhys! Your expression is priceless."

The midwife laughed. "I am not certain your lord husband will survive two more deliveries," she teased and Rhys could not hold back his smile.

He claimed Catherine's hand and kissed her knuckles. "Whatsoever the lady desires, so it shall be."

"I shall send you 'round to share that view with my husband," the midwife said and they laughed together. "Now, my lady, time for a change for you." The women bustled around the chamber with fierce efficiency, easing Catherine from the bed that they might change the linens. Foster helped Catherine and busily washed her. Rhys would have retreated, but the midwife's apprentice offered him the swaddled child. He accepted the tiny burden with wonder, noting the dark auburn hair on the child's head and the perfection of those tiny fingers.

His son.

Rhys found his throat tight.

"Right as rain, he is," the midwife said.

He carried the boy to the window, where the full moon's light shone down on the garden square opposite. The silverly light touched the boy's face, making him look like the miracle Rhys knew him to be. He heard the bells ring at the closest church and realized it was midnight. He bent and kissed the forehead of the newly arrived infant, who squirmed and grimaced. The boy's face reddened as he mustered his strength and he gave another more vigorous cry, his tiny fist shaking.

"I know what he wants," Catherine said softly and Rhys turned to find her arms open. Her clean nightgown was unfastened at the front and Foster had combed her hair. She looked like an angel, though it was clear she had no intention of joining their numbers as yet. "I have been thinking of names," she said as she nestled the boy close. She cast Rhys a look. "What was your father's name?"

"Nicholas."

"Oh, I like that," she said with approval. "And my father is Edmond. Nicholas Edmond Bettencourt," she whispered to the infant. The babe gurgled then took the nipple, obviously with enough force that Catherine caught her breath.

"Perfect," Rhys said, and he meant more than the choice of name. He would give her the parure before Christmas Day and admire it upon her, but for the moment, he would treasure a gift that could not be bought, the health of his beloved wife and son.

It was more than sufficient to make his life complete.

Catherine looked up at him and smiled, a sight of which he would never tire. She had undermined his convictions at their wedding with that smile, and now she proved herself aright. There was no curse, just as she had insisted.

On the contrary, as he settled beside his lady wife to watch her nurse their son, Rhys Bettencourt felt blessed indeed.

~

THE MASQUERADE OF THE MARCHIONESS

THE LADIES' ESSENTIAL GUIDE TO THE ART OF SEDUCTION #2

Philomena Wright, Marchioness of Arlingview, is universally admired for her intellect, good sense and charitable efforts on behalf of widows and orphans. She seems to have every advantage, but secretly desires that her dashing husband, the one person indifferent to her accomplishments, would notice her. The issue, clearly, is that she is too dull to hold his attention—when she is offered the opportunity, Philomena cannot resist the temptation of pursuing her husband in disguise.

Garrett Wright misses the purpose—and the peril— of his work as a spy during the war and is bored with his long-time disguise as a reckless rake. When he accepts an assignment to identify a jewel thief preying upon London society, he meets a mysterious masked beauty kindles his passion with her bold touch. Could she be the thief? Garrett becomes determined to both possess and unveil the temptress, whatever the cost.

Philomena and Garrett's game of cat-and-mouse enthralls them both, but when Philomena is revealed, Garrett fears his wife has another secret. Will catching the thief place his beloved wife in jeopardy? Forced to choose between honor and love, how will Garrett find a means to fulfill his duty and secure a happy future with Philomena?

The Masquerade of the Marchioness
The Ladies' Essential Guide to the Art of Seduction #2
Coming November 2022!

~

ABOUT THE AUTHOR

Deborah Cooke sold her first book in 1992, a medieval romance called **Romance of the Rose** published under her pseudonym Claire Delacroix. Since then, she has published over ninety novels in a wide variety of sub-genres, including historical romance, contemporary romance, paranormal romance, fantasy romance, time-travel romance, women's fiction, paranormal young adult and fantasy with romantic elements. She has published under the names Claire Delacroix, Claire Cross and Deborah Cooke. **The Beauty**, part of her successful Bride Quest series of historical romances, was her first title to land on the *New York Times* List of Bestselling Books. Her books routinely appear on other bestseller lists and have won numerous awards. In 2009, she was the writer-in-residence at the Toronto Public Library, the first time the library has hosted a residency focused on the romance genre. In 2012, she was honored to receive the Romance Writers of America's Mentor of the Year Award.

Currently, she writes paranormal romances featuring dragon shape shifter heroes under the name Deborah Cooke. She also writes medieval romances as Claire Delacroix. Deborah lives in Canada with her husband and family, as well as far too many unfinished knitting projects.

Visit Deborah's websites to learn more about her books:

DeborahCooke.com

Delacroix.net

THE ROGUE
THE SCOUNDREL
THE WARRIOR

The Jewels of Kinfairlie
THE BEAUTY BRIDE
THE ROSE RED BRIDE
THE SNOW WHITE BRIDE
The Ballad of Rosamunde

The True Love Brides
THE RENEGADE'S HEART
THE HIGHLANDER'S CURSE
THE FROST MAIDEN'S KISS
THE WARRIOR'S PRIZE

The Brides of Inverfyre
THE MERCENARY'S BRIDE
THE RUNAWAY BRIDE

The Bride Quest
THE PRINCESS
THE DAMSEL
THE HEIRESS
THE COUNTESS
THE BEAUTY
THE TEMPTRESS

Harlequin Historicals
UNICORN BRIDE
PEARL BEYOND PRICE

www.ingramcontent.com/pod-product-compliance
Lightning Source LLC
Chambersburg PA
CBHW030957210726
48290CB00007B/2345